Los Espíritus

ISBN: 978-1-951226-00-8

Edited and typeset by Nathaniel Kennon Perkins
Cover art by Chris Hunt
Story Consultant by Jenny Deller

Published by Trident Press
940 Pearl St.
Boulder, CO 80302
tridentcafe.com/trident-press

Los Espíritus

Original Screenplay by

JOSH HYDE

Trident Press
Boulder, CO

INT. MIDDLE SCHOOL CLASSROOM - MORNING

OLIVIA, mid-30's, dresses stylish, yet respectful. The classroom is empty as she organizes desks and chairs. The walls are painted in a rainbow pattern, bright and inviting. Beanbags surround the reading area, a corner with large bookshelves filled with books for 6th graders.

Olivia cleans up the "reading corner," arranging the beanbags.

She sits on her desk, scanning the room, taking a drink of water, setting the glass on the table. Done.

EXT. CAR IN PARKING LOT OF MIDDLE SCHOOL - MORNING

LAWRENCE, mid 40's, parks his car in a visitor's parking spot. He's wearing a jacket, tie, and collared shirt, tucked in. Clean-shaven.

He double-checks his outfit in the rearview mirror. Contemporary, yet conservative.

Lawrence grabs a bouquet of flowers, hiding an engagement ring in a jacket pocket.

EXT. SCHOOL ENTRANCE - CONTINUOUS

Lawrence enters the school. Ready.

INT. MIDDLE SCHOOL - CONTINUOUS

Lawrence continues down a hallway into an office. He signs in, holding up the flowers, smiling to an OLDER SECRETARY, "Hello."

OLDER SECRETARY: For me? You're so sweet.

Lawrence takes a single flower from the bouquet, handing it to the Older Secretary.

LAWRENCE: That one's for you.

OLDER SECRETARY: (smelling the flower) Are they for Ms. Swope?

Lawrence shakes his head, "No."

OLDER SECRETARY: (CONT'D) Ms. Galbreth?

LAWRENCE: (smiling) Ms. Mattingly.

The Secretary pauses, thinking of another teacher.

OLDER SECRETARY: The quiet one?

Lawrence nods, "I like the quiet ones."

OLDER SECRETARY: (CONT'D) You're here for Ms. Mouse. Sign here.

Lawrence signs his name and reason for visit.

SECRETARY: The kids love her, but she's a quiet. Room 222.

Lawrence smiles, thanks, exiting the office.

SECRETARY: (CONT'D) Good luck, Mr. Mouse.

INT. MIDDLE SCHOOL CLASSROOM - CONTINUOUS

Olivia looks through her notes as Lawrence appears in the doorway. He pauses, looking at her. She's beautiful. He takes the ring out of his pocket, looking at it one last time, opening the door.

Olivia looks up, surprised.

OLIVIA: Don't you have class?

Lawrence smiles, shaking his head, "No."

LAWRENCE: They have a project on the American Revolution.

She sees the flowers.

OLIVIA: Are those part of the American Revolution?

Lawrence hands the bouquet to Olivia.

She smells the flowers, searching for a place to put them, finding the glass of water on the table. She puts the flowers in the water, arranging them.

Lawrence kneels on the ground, taking the ring out of his pocket, holding it up.

She holds up the glass of flowers, finding Lawrence on his knees.

She stops as her eyes find the ring.

LAWRENCE: I know you don't have a traditional family, but I want you to be part of mine. Will you marry me?

Olivia swells with excitement, looking into his eyes, slowly nodding, "Yes."

INT. HOUSE OF LOS ESPIRITUS - SIMULTANEOUS

SAMANTHA, early 70's, a fit and sturdy senior citizen, leads a group meditation with three older women dressed in flowing clothes.

SAMANTHA: Let the world in with your breath.

She INHALES deeply, setting the pace.

SAMANTHA: (CONT'D) And exhale your soul to play.

All of the women EXHALE together.

A cell phone VIBRATES, announcing a call.

SAMANTHA: (CONT'D) Keep breathing.

Samantha picks up the phone.

SAMANTHA: (CONT'D):It's working. Look who's calling.

She holds up the phone. It reads, "Olivia-Darling."

CAMILLE, 75, an African American grandma wearing yoga pants and a t-shirt reading, "Liberate Yourself."

CAMILLE: Answer it.

MARGO, 78, a Jewish grandma meditating in a yoga position with a rainbow-colored outfit.

MARGO: Of all our children, Olivia's is my favorite.

CARMEN: Tell her we say hi.

CARMEN, 70, a short Asian grandma, waives burning incense in circles around her chakras, cleansing them. She's wearing loose fitting pants and a panda t-shirt. Carmen waives the incense around the cell phone as Samantha answers it.

OLIVIA: (V.O.) How you doing Sammy?

SAMANTHA: (into phone) Group meditation. We're trying to get the souls to come out and play. How's your soul, love?

Samantha waives her hand, clearing the incense smoke.

INT. MIDDLE SCHOOL CLASSROOM - SIMULTANEOUS

Olivia stands, looking out the window. Children PLAY outside.

OLIVIA: (into phone) My soul is happy. Lawrence proposed.

INT. HOUSE OF LOS ESPIRITUS - SIMULTANEOUS

Samantha is quiet, unsure.

SAMANTHA: (into phone) The professor is the winner, huh? Makes sense, you both teach. (pausing) I have to say one thing and then you can ask me whatever you called to ask. And remember...

OLIVIA: (V.O.) Sammy, I remember. You're the reason I'm here.

Samantha smiles, listening.

SAMANTHA: (into phone) Not that one. The other one. I'm older than you and I've seen it all.

OLIVIA (V.O.) Another personal favorite.

SAMANTHA (into phone): Statistically, you're going to outlive him by four years. Men are simple beings, and if you don't watch out, they'll control you with their small minds. No matter how much you love him.

Camille, Carmen, and Margo listen, nodding their heads in agreement from meditation position.

SAMANTHA: (into phone) That's why there are no male organizations like Espiritus. Women last longer than men, love.

INT. MIDDLE SCHOOL CLASSROOM - SIMULTANEOUS

Olivia paces around the room.

OLIVIA: (into phone) That's why I love you. Can I ask my question now?

SAMANTHA: (O.S.) I'm ready, love.

OLIVIA: (into phone) Can you help me plan the wedding? I need your spirit to be here to make sure things don't go wrong. Olivia waits for the answer.

SAMANTHA: (O.S.) You know what being part of Los Espiritus means.

OLIVIA: (into phone) I'll be fine when you're gone. I think the wedding will help you transcend.
It'll be our good-bye.

INT. HOUSE OF LOS ESPIRITUS - SIMULTANEOUS

Samantha makes eye contact with Margo, Carmen, and Camille.

SAMANTHA: You're sweet, love. I can almost feel the other side. Planning a wedding might ground me back into my body. (whispering) I can leave my body, and I even can move stuff with my aura.

INT. MIDDLE SCHOOL CLASSROOM - SIMULTANEOUS

Olivia stops pacing.

SAMANTHA: (V.O.) I don't want the extra emotions to confuse my spirit on its journey.

She looks out the window at a playground full of kids.

OLIVIA: (into phone) The wedding is my last request. And then you can transcend. I'll even help.

INT. HOUSE OF LOS ESPIRITUS -SIMULTANEOUS

Carmen, Camille, and Margo smile, eavesdropping on the phone call. Still meditating.

CARMEN: (whispering) I love weddings.

SAMANTHA: (into phone) Death isn't gonna sneak up on me. We're gonna ambush it from above. All you have to do is come to my wake.

INT. MIDDLE SCHOOL CLASSROOM - SIMULTANEOUS

OLIVIA: (into phone) Stop it. You're my mother and father rolled into a super grandma. I'm helping you transcend and you're going to plan the wedding with me.

INT. HOUSE OF LOS ESPIRITUS - SIMULTANEOUS

Carmen, Margo, and Camille overhear "plan the wedding," and meditation is over.

They stir out of full embodiment, calmly swarming Samantha.

CARMEN: I'll help.

MARGO: We can have a non-denominational wedding.

CAMILLE: I always wanted to go to a Buddhist wedding before we transcended.

Samantha is still on the phone, listening to Camille, Margo, and Carmen.

INT. MIDDLE SCHOOL CLASSROOM - SIMULTANEOUS

OLIVIA: (into phone) I need my wedding to be our final moment together...Before you reincarnate.

INT. HOUSE OF LOS ESPIRITUS - SIMULTANEOUS

SAMANTHA: (into phone) We're not reincarnating. We're passing through the wheels of birth, life, and death to transcend the human plane. Forever.

INT. MIDDLE SCHOOL CLASSROOM - SIMULTANEOUS

OLIVIA: (into phone) But what happens if you miss a wheel?

Silence.

SAMANTHA: (V.O.) I guess reincarnation.

INT. HOUSE OF LOS ESPIRITUS - SIMULTANEOUS

Samantha and Los Espiritus are quiet, listening.

SAMANTHA: (into phone) It's all a mystery, technically.

CAMILLE: (whispering) I need a wedding before I go.

Samantha walks away from Camille, Carmen, and Margo.

They follow her.

MARGO: It'll be our final mission.

Carmen dances in place, waiving the incense in big circles.

CARMEN: (singing) We're going to a wedding. We're going to a wedding.

Samantha finds Carmen, Margo, and Camille's eyes, "It'll be fun."

SAMANTHA: (into phone) Los Espiritus want to help.

Margo CLAPS her hands, celebrating.

INT. SAMANTHA'S ROOM - NIGHT

The room is sparse. Clean. At one end is a meditation shrine and the other, a small bed.

The meditation shrine has a small Buddha surrounded by candles. Olivia's photo sits on the shrine as Samantha looks at it.

Samantha packs a bag of clothes and another bag of spiritual tools: yoga mat, tai chi shoes, a gift box with a ribbon, Buddhist prayer flags, a Buddhist head dress, and various silver and crystal relics.

INT. CAMILLE'S ROOM - SIMULTANEOUS

The walls are covered in saffron colored sheets. The lair of a "monk-tress."

Camille holds up a large metal Buddhist ceremonial relic.

CAMILLE: (chanting) Ommanipadmehum.

She puts it in a carry on bag stuffed with meditation pillows, crystals, acupuncture needles, and tai chi shoes.

INT. MARGO'S ROOM - SIMULTANEOUS

The walls start in red, shifting to orange-yellow-green-blue-indigo-violet. The rainbow engulfs the room.

Incense smoke rises from an alter as Margo bows to a star of David with an Ohm symbol in the middle.

She packs a deck of Kabbalah-based tarot cards, a crystal cross, a Tibetan singing bowl, and a lot of incense.

INT. CARMEN'S ROOM - SIMULTANEOUS

The original Buddhist swastika hangs over a golden Buddha statue.

A sword slices through the air as Carmen gracefully executes a tai chi move. Buddhist prayer beads hang off her wrist.

Carmen's eyes are closed as the blade passes by her face.

Her eyes open. Ready.

EXT. SAMANTHA'S DRIVEWAY - MORNING

Los Espiritus pack up an older-model, boxy Volvo station wagon with their bags and spiritual tools: foam wands, meditation cushions, swords, etc.

MARGO: What if he's a dud?

SAMANTHA: He's got a career. I think he does cardio.

CAMILLE: Does he meditate?

MARGO: Men don't meditate.

CARMEN: Stop being negative. Some men meditate.

Samantha shakes her head, "No."

SAMANTHA: I think he teaches Western Civilization.

INT. UNIVERSITY CLASSROOM - NIGHT

Lawrence stands in front of a small graduate class.

LAWRENCE: The early Americas were a vicious place, where the original Americans and the settlers battled savagely for survival. For the settlers, persecuted for religion, they found the original inhabitants of America and decided to tame the savages and their land.

A female student, 28, nerdy and attractive, SOPHIA, eyes him.

INT. FRONT OF CLASSROOM - LATER

The class is over. Lawrence organizes lecture notes as Sophia approaches the desk.

SOPHIA: Dr. Levine, I was getting my thesis committee together, and I need a chair.

Sophia smiles at Lawrence, flirting.

LAWRENCE: What's your thesis?

SOPHIA: (smiling, proud of herself) I want to call it...
(gathering her thoughts, inspired)
"Colonial Love: Marriage and Courting in the early Americas."

Lawrence smiles at her bright mind.

SOPHIA: There was nothing. If you were a woman... (consuming Lawrence with her eyes) Survival depended on the man who chose you. What were the most important qualities? Did religion enslave woman? What was a date like?

LAWRENCE: It's... (thinking of the words) different.

SOPHIA: That's why I need you to be my chair. You have the best access to early American archives in the department. And you know how to bring history to life.

Lawrence blushes, feeling validated.

LAWRENCE: At least you've thought it out.

Sophia nods, "I've thought it out."

LAWRENCE: Can you meet tomorrow?

Sophia smiles, "Tomorrow is perfect."

INT. OLIVIA'S KITCHEN - NIGHT

Olivia makes dinner in the kitchen as Lawrence looks at a computer.

Images of happy OLDER WOMEN doing spiritual group activities fill the screen.

LAWRENCE: Any member of a group named "Los Espiritus" makes me nervous.

Lawrence clicks on a video. It plays.

VIDEO NARRATOR: Los Espiritus is a group for women to transcend life with integrity and hope. Globally, women outlive men. After your partner dies, the female journey continues to transcend the human form.

A time lapse of a caterpillar making a cocoon and slowly emerging as a butterfly.

Lawrence LAUGHS.

OLIVIA: Everybody needs a hobby.

Various shots of older women doing group activities: yoga, tai chi in a pool, meditating.

VIDEO NARRATOR: We focus on a variety of reincarnation traditions. Our goal is to overcome reincarnation and find enlightenment before the physical body dies. Together we will transcend the wheels of Samsara... The endless cycle of life, death, and re-birth.

A group of Older Woman do tai chi, silhouetted by the sun.

The image fades into a title, the url "www.espiritus.com."

Lawrence and Olivia look at each other.

LAWRENCE: I don't think it's a hobby. It's a cult.

OLIVIA: What else do you want them to do?

LAWRENCE: Be normal and hide in their houses until they're dead.

Olivia looks at him, "That's horrible."

OLIVIA: What's wrong with meditation and tai chi? A little incense? Everyone needs love.

Lawrence is quiet.

OLIVIA: Spirituality intimidates you.

LAWRENCE: I'm not intimidated. I've just never met a single Espiritu and tomorrow I'm gonna meet the whole western Colorado chapter.

Olivia pacifies Lawrence with a kiss.

OLIVIA: It's only the Boulder Chapter.

LAWRENCE: Now I'm intimidated.

INT. OLIVIA'S BEDROOM - MORNING

Lawrence and Olivia slowly wake up, hearing VOICES outside.

CARMEN: (O.S.) I'm ready for tai chi.

EXT. OLIVIA'S DRIVEWAY - CONTINUOUS

The boxy Volvo station wagon is parked in the driveway.
Samantha, Carmen, Margo, and Camille stretch their arms and legs.

MARGO: We have to see Olivia first.

INT. OLIVIA'S BEDROOM - CONTINUOUS

Olivia looks out the window, watching Los Espiritus.

They're like a confused group of children, moving in every direction, which somehow leads to the front door.

Olivia quickly dressing up, exiting the bedroom.
Lawrence watches Los Espiritus through the window, half awake.

LAWRENCE: (to himself) They seem harmless.

INT. OLIVIA'S KITCHEN - MORNING

Boiling hot water is poured into gourds filled with yerba mate.

Carmen picks up the gourd, sipping out of a metal straw.

Olivia and Lawrence drink coffee at the head of the table.

Samantha, Carmen, Margo, and Camille sit around the table. Enjoying the yerba mate.

LAWRENCE: I want a wedding in a church. It'll make my parents happy. And it's the easiest thing to do for us.

Lawrence puts his hand on Olivia's knee, making eye contact with her, agreeing.

Carmen's eyes roll, disapproving.

Camille nods, "He said church."

Samantha smiles at Lawrence.

SAMANTHA: That's definitely one of the options on the table. A simple...

LAWRENCE: Catholic...

SAMANTHA: Church wedding.

Samantha looks at Olivia.

SAMANTHA: A simple Catholic church wedding. (Putting on a smile) Lawrence, men are funny creatures. You're marrying a piece of the universe that completes your tiny, tiny...

CAMILLE: Tiny.

SAMANTHA: Tiny soul. And you want it to be simple.

Lawrence nods, naive and controlling.

LAWRENCE: The wedding can be simple.

MARGO: It can be so simple, we don't even need a church.

SAMANTHA:Nature.

CARMEN: Family.

CAMILLE:Lovers.

LAWRENCE: That might be too simple...
(turning to Olivia)
...but I'll let you decide. I'm not good at these kind of things.

SAMANTHA: Lawrence, you have decided what you want. What does Olivia want?

Lawrence holds Olivia's hand.

LAWRENCE: I'm sorry, I wasn't...

OLIVIA: (cutting him off) I know, we're not going to agree on everything, but I want this to be a way for Lawrence to get to know you.

Samantha and Lawrence look at each other, faking smiles.

LAWRENCE: A simple church wedding...

SAMANTHA: (cutting him off) Will definitely be one of

the options. Our goal is to make the wedding special. There's only one Olivia.

CAMILLE: And there's only one Lawrence.

MARGO: And you two coming together will only happen once.

CARMEN: (holding up one finger) Once.

Olivia smiles at the compliment, kissing Lawrence.

Samantha makes eye contact with Camille, Margo, and Carmen, "I don't like him."

INT. FRONT DOOR - CONTINUOUS

Lawrence leaves the house as Olivia kisses him good-bye.

Samantha observes Olivia's fairy tale.

INT. LIVING ROOM - CONTINUOUS

Samantha makes eye contact with Margo, Carmen, and Camille.

MARGO: (whispering) He's bad.

Carmen and Camille nod, "He's a douche."

CAMILLE: He's so douchey, he can't do cardio.

CARMEN: It's his brain. He's all brain and no... (thinking of the words) no...

CAMILLE:Intuition.

MARGO: Action.

SAMANTHA: Love.

Carmen searches for the words, nodding her head.

CARMEN: Balls...No balls.

SAMANTHA: Let's clear this place.

Huge smiles run across Carmen, Margo, and Camille's faces. Ready.

INT. BEDROOM - CONTINUOUS

Carmen unzips her bag, flipping it open.

She takes inventory of the spiritual weapons.

Various incense bundles. Sticks of palo santo. A saffron scarf. And a tai chi sword.

INT. LIVING ROOM - CONTINUOUS

Margo and Camille set out a condor feather, a purple bag with the symbol of Rah, a bundle of sage, and a large abalone shell on the coffee table.

INT. WALKING THROUGH EVERY ROOM IN THE HOUSE - CONTINUOUS

Carmen opens windows, smudging the whole house with sage and palo santo.

CARMEN: Bye-bye.

INT. BEDROOM - CONTINUOUS

Samantha unpacks her bags, finding a small box wrapped with a bow.

The bow is purple with suns and moons.

INT. KITCHEN - CONTINUOUS

Margo sets up a card reading on the kitchen table. Samantha, Carmen, Camille, and Olivia sit down.

SAMANTHA: We got you something, love. (Handing her the box) Open it.

Olivia takes it, surprised. Unwrapping the gift.

It's a used tarot deck.

OLIVIA: Where'd you find these?

SAMANTHA: Margo found them in your old room.

Olivia opens up the worn box, anxious to meet an old friend.

She shuffles the cards. It's second nature.

SAMANTHA: You were a natural.

OLIVIA: (Smiling) I'm a little rusty.

MARGO: Let's read your aura.

Margo scans Olivia up and down, squinting her eyes.

MARGO: Too...yellow.

Los Espiritus look Olivia over, agreeing. Too yellow.

CARMEN: Ratna.

Carmen pokes Olivia's skin, "Definitely, ratna."

OLIVIA: Ratna?

SAMANTHA: It's a Buddhist thing, love.

INT. KITCHEN - MOMENTS LATER

Margo removes a deck of cards from the fuzzy bag with the symbol of Ra.

She sets the cards in front of Olivia.

MARGO: The Tarot was almost lost, but my people preserved it. In this deck each card represents every possible phenomena in nature.

Olivia holds the cards, focusing her intention, shuffling the cards.

MARGO: When you're ready, divide the stack in two.
Olivia cuts the cards in two stacks. Ready.

CARMEN:One stack is the yin and the other is the yang stack.

CAMILLE: That's why we do tai chi.

OLIVIA: (pointing at a stack) That's the yin stack.

Margo hands Olivia the yin stack.

MARGO: Shuffle and focus on setting things in motion. When you're done, hand me the top and bottom cards.

Olivia shuffles the stack, taking a breath.

She hands Margo the bottom and top cards.

Margo builds the card layout, setting the first two cards face down.

MARGO: Do the same thing with the yang stack. Focus on receiving, pulling opportunities to you.

SAMANTHA: Trust yourself, love.

Olivia closes her eyes, receiving, shuffling the cards.

She opens her eyes, pulling the top and bottom cards, handing them to Margo.

Margo sets the new cards face down. The cards form a square.

MARGO: Now combine yin and yang. And charge them up.

Olivia combines the two stacks, shuffling a couple times.

MARGO: And spread them on the table.

Olivia fans out the cards on the table.

MARGO: Pick one end as the head and the other will be the feet.

Olivia points at one end.

OLIVIA: That's the head.

MARGO: Take one card from the head. And another card from the foot.

Olivia's fingers scan the cards, selecting a card from the head, handing it to Margo.

Her fingers pick a card from the feet side, holding it up.

Margo takes the final cards, putting them in the layout. She closes her eyes, circling her hands over the cards.

MARGO: (Opening her eyes) We're ready.

Olivia fidgets, nervous.

CAMILLE: Don't be nervous, honey. Your destiny is about to wink at you.

Margo flips over the first card. It's a priest.

SAMANTHA: That's Lawrence.

MARGO: Shhhh. Stop projecting.

Margo holds the card, taking a deep breathe.

MARGO:(Closing her eyes) It's the Hierophant. This is what is currently happening in your life. There is something with rigid structure in your life.

Margo moves her head in circles, channeling.

MARGO: It's an ideology. On the surface it seems fine, but when you really look at it... (nodding her head) it doesn't fit.

Margo opens her eyes. Silent.

Olivia looks at Samantha, absorbing the meaning. Margo turns over the next card. It's a Hanging Man.

CARMEN: Damn, it's Lawrence.

MARGO: Stop projecting.

Margo takes a deep breath.

MARGO: If you need clarity, just think about the confusion, shuffle the extra cards, and pick one. The card you pick will help you figure it out.

Olivia nods, "I need some clarity."

She SHUFFLES the cards, looking at the Hanged Man. She draws a card, flipping it over. It's the Lovers.

CAMILLE: Mmm, Mmm.

Everybody is quiet.

MARGO: It's Lawrence.
(thinking of the right words)
You need to change your relationship to him.

OLIVIA: What does that mean?

Los Espiritus look at Olivia.

MARGO: Sometimes relationships free us and sometimes they trap us.

Olivia is quiet. She flips over the next card. It's an Old Man holding a lamp, the Hermit.

MARGO: You have to give and receive. The Hermit finds

stillness, learns from older generations and completes all unfinished business.

Olivia is upset, shuffling the cards. She picks a card, hoping to find clarity.

She sets it down, face up. The card of Change, decorated with a yin and yang symbol.

OLIVIA: Great.

MARGO: Whatever is going to happen, it's gonna happen in four weeks. That's an awful powerful card, love.

Olivia shifts in her seat.

OLIVIA: (looking at Samantha) Is this why you came?

SAMANTHA: We didn't do anything.

OLIVIA: You just told me Lawrence is controlling and I need to cancel the wedding.

SAMANTHA: We just told you the meaning of the cards. It's not up to us how you read the cards.

OLIVIA: I know how the cards work, Samantha.

Olivia stands up from the table.

OLIVIA: This isn't happening. This is my life.

She paces around the kitchen.

OLIVIA: You're not here to help me find Mr. Right. You're here to plan the wedding.

Olivia glares at Samantha.

OLIVIA: I'm done.

SAMANTHA: The cards don't lie.

OLIVIA: Humans do...I've heard it a thousand times, Sammy.

SAMANTHA: Look at us. (Staring down Olivia) Take a deep, deep breath...

Olivia slows down, emotions calming.

SAMANTHA: And a good hard look. Maybe even stare.

Olivia stares at Margo, Carmen, and Camille.

SAMANTHA: Where's Margo's life partner? And Carmen's?

Carmen smiles at Olivia.

CARMEN: Heart attack. He only liked cardio.

SAMANTHA: Where's the "love" of Camille's life?

Camille looks at Olivia.

CAMILLE: I wish he was dead. She was a 19-year-old Ukrainian he met at Applebee's. (Rolling her eyes) When he was "traveling" for work.

SAMANTHA: Margo?

MARGO: (remembering) I had so many lovers... (smiling) I outlived them all. Woman have better genetics.

OLIVIA: I know you all love me, but...

CAMILLE: It's not about love. It's about illusion. He thinks you're going to heaven.

CARMEN: Heaven's not real.

MARGO: (cutting her off) Your soul is gonna get stuck, honey.

OLIVIA: I know you don't want me reincarnating by myself, but...

CARMEN: Transcending.

OLIVIA: Whatever. I'm not one of you. I don't want to transcend. My soul wants a family, love, maybe some grand kids.

Samantha, Carmen, Margo, and Camille listen.

OLIVIA: Thanks for the yellow aura and card reading, but I don't need help replacing Lawrence.

Los Espiritus are quiet, guilty.

SAMANTHA: We're not trying to...

OLIVIA: (interrupting) If you're not going to help plan the wedding... You can leave in the morning.

Samantha, Carmen, Camille, and Margo look at each other, eventually making eye contact with Olivia.

SAMANTHA: You can't ignore the message, even if...

OLIVIA: (interrupting) I'm not a kid, Samantha...And I don't believe in messages from cards anymore. I'm marrying Lawrence.

Olivia WALKS out of the kitchen, SLAMMING the door to her bedroom.

Samantha, Carmen, Camille, and Margo sit in SILENCE at the table.

Carmen has an idea, about to speak, but stops in the name of SILENCE.

SAMANTHA: I can't do this. It's her life and if I get emotionally attached I won't be able to transcend.

CARMEN: We can't apologize for the cards.

CAMILLE: Does it really matter?

MARGO: The cards spoke.

CARMEN: Have they ever been wrong?

Margo shakes her head, "Never."

Carmen, Camille, and Margo make eye contact with Samantha.

SAMANTHA: Just because someone gets a glimpse of the future, doesn't mean they're ready for it.

Samantha, Camille, Carmen, and Margo nod, agreeing.

Their eyes find the remaining cards on the table. Samantha

We might as well be thorough.
Margo flips over the remaining cards.

The moon. The universe. The fool.

They smile at the cards, "We're in for a ride."

Carmen pulls out her cell phone, taking a photo for evidence.

INT. OLIVIA'S BEDROOM - CONTINOUS

Olivia is facedown on the bed. There's a KNOCK on the door.

Olivia is motionless. Unresponsive.

There's another KNOCK on the door.

OLIVIA: Leave me alone.

SAMANTHA: (O.S.) (speaking through the door) If you want to marry him...We'll help you.

MARGO: (O.S.) (speaking through the door) We don't like

him, but we love you.

Olivia turns over, listening.

CAMILLE: (O.S.) (speaking through the door) We'll pretend we like him.

SAMANTHA: (O.S.) (speaking through the door) When do we start pretending?

Olivia smiles, feeling the love.

INT. OLIVIA'S BEDROOM/BATHROOM - NIGHT

Lawrence puts on pajamas as Olivia grades papers in bed.

OLIVIA: They almost left today.

Lawrence laughs.

OLIVIA: We did a card reading and...

LAWRENCE: (interrupting) Are we doomed?
(making eye contact)
Forever.

OLIVIA: And ever.

Lawrence is dressed in pajamas with matching tops and bottoms.

LAWRENCE: I thought I was being nice.

OLIVA: Just keep an open mind. And remember, they're overly sensitive.

Lawrence gets into bed.

LAWRENCE: What's wrong with a church wedding?

He looks at Olivia as she grades her papers.

LAWRENCE: It's the easiest option.

Lawrence kisses Olivia on the forehead.

OLIVIA: Just be patient. They mean well.

LAWRENCE: Can we have a signal for when we're entering the "sensitive" zone?

Olivia looks at Lawrence, "A signal?"

LAWRENCE: They're a force of nature.

OLIVIA: Maybe...

Olivia's hands do tai chi circles.

LAWRENCE: We need something subtle. Maybe...

His face erupts into extreme fear as his eyes bulge, calling for help.

Olivia laughs, attracted.

INT. KITCHEN - DAY

The table is filled with plates of eclectic food. The plates are numbered, 1-4.

SAMANTHA: Each plate is a wedding theme. Try them and pick your favorites.

Olivia and Lawrence sample foods from the plates.

LAWRENCE: Plate 1 is my favorite.

MARGO: In the Kabbalah, number 1 represents leadership and management.

Margo leans into Samantha, whispering in her ear.

MARGO: Minus a big ego.

Lawrence notices Margo whispering.

LAWRENCE: No secrets.

SAMANTHA: Don't worry. It's a good thing.

Olivia smiles.

OLIVIA: What does 3 mean?

Margo smiles.

MARGO: You will be successful in new endeavors.

Margo pauses, thinking of the words.

SAMANTHA: You see the good in people.

OLIVIA: What're the bad parts?

Margo smiles.

MARGO: You're naive, yet persistent.

CARMEN: The good news is plate 1 represents the food at the nature wedding.

CAMILLE: Plate 3 is the food at the Buddhist wedding.

CARMEN: I'm proud of you Lawrence.
(winking at him)
The nature wedding is my idea.

Lawrence smiles, "Thanks," happy to be accepted.

INT. LIVING ROOM - MOMENTS LATER

A cloud of smoke rises from a smoldering piece of Palo Santo wood as Carmen appears.

CARMEN: Close your eyes.

Samantha, Margo, Camille, and Olivia close their eyes.

Lawrence awkwardly closes his eyes. Uncomfortable.

CARMEN: Nature is everywhere.

EXT. GREEN VALLEY WITH FLOWING RIVER - DAY

A blue sky fills with clouds.

CARMEN: (V.O.) Sky. Clouds. Trees. A valley. A river.

Wind BREATHES through the treetops.

A river FLOWS through the valley.

CARMEN: (V.O.) The ceremony will be near the sacred waters.

Camille, Samantha, and Margo smile, standing in the valley.

Olivia inhales the wind. She's in the valley.

INT. LIVING ROOM - DAY

Lawrence looks confused, eyes closed. He cracks one eye, scanning the group. He's not in the valley.

He closes his eyes, visualizing harder.

CARMEN: The bride and groom are on opposite sides of the river for the ceremony. When the ceremony is over, you'll meet in the middle for the ring exchange.

LAWRENCE: What about our shoes?

Images of Lawrence's feet, wearing various shoes as he walks through the stream.

CARMEN: You're not wearing shoes.

Lawrence opens his eyes, frustrated, "I can't see it."

CARMEN: The reception will be in the large cabin.

LAWRENCE: We can't have the reception in a cabin.

Samantha, Camille, and Margo open their eyes. The vision is over.

CARMEN: Cabins go great with nature.

LAWRENCE: I have a lot of family flying in and they're hotel people. They want to be close to bars and restaurants.

OLIVIA: Lawrence's mom is a Marriott Silver Elite member.

CARMEN: Applebee's and Marriott don't fit with the nature theme.

LAWRENCE: My family doesn't eat at Applebee's.

MARGO: If they stay at Marriott's, they eat at Applebee's.

LAWRENCE: What does that mean?

CAMILLE: Strip clubs. My ex stayed at Marriott's, ate Applebee's, and loved strip clubs.

OLIVIA: Lawrence isn't your ex-husband.

Camille is quiet, giving Lawrence the evil eye, "Am I lying?"

LAWRENCE: What?

CAMILLE: Tell me your not going to a strip club.

LAWRENCE: I mean, I don't want to go. My uncles want to take me.

OLIVIA: (rolling her eyes) We talked about the strip club already.

CAMILLE: Olivia, do you eat Applebee's?

OLIVIA: No, I don't eat Applebee's.

CARMEN: Good.

Samantha, Carmen, Margo, and Camille look at each other, frustrated by the strip club idea.

They take a DEEP BREATH in. EXHALING together.

OLIVIA: What if the ceremony is in the park by the Denver Zoo? And the reception can be in the mountains overlooking the city.

Samantha, Carmen, Margo, and Camille look at Lawrence, compromising.

He shakes his head, "I don't like it."

LAWRENCE: It seems complicated.

Olivia shakes her head, "I don't like it, either."

OLIVIA: It's not a good fit. What are the other ideas?

Carmen bites her tongue as the nature wedding fails.

INT. MARGO'S BEDROOM - CONTINUOUS

Margo picks up something under a sheet.

The sheet has an ohm symbol on it.

INT. LIVING ROOM - CONTINUOUS

Margo sets down the object covered by a sheet.

MARGO:The next idea is a fusion of all religions.

She pulls the sheet off, revealing a detailed, 3D model of the fusion wedding.

CARMEN: Holy shit.

Carmen picks up one of the mini chairs, while Samantha plays with the mini-alter.

Margo holds a wooden tai chi sword as a pointer.

MARGO: It's sunset. We build a nomadic circular tent for a grand feast.

Margo points out the nomadic tent.

MARGO: The ceremony and the banquet take place in the

tent. (pointing out the mini-cars) And a car service for people to get back to their hotels. (pointing out smaller tents) And more tents for people who want to stay the night.

OLIVIA: I'd like to have a sleep over on the night of the wedding. That sounds fun.

Olivia looks at Lawrence for his approval.

LAWRENCE: So, it's like a huge party?

Margo points to a large fire pit.

MARGO: The bonfire will be here.

LAWRENCE: What about the parents who have kids?

MARGO: We can add a baby-sitting tent...

The tai chi sword points out an empty part of land on the model.

MARGO: Here.

LAWRENCE: Can a priest be the official? My parents need to see a priest or something resembling a cross to feel like it's official.

CAMILLE: Who cares what they want? It's your day.

LAWRENCE: It's easier for Olivia to do what she wants because she doesn't have any parents. (looking at Olivia, holding her hand)Samantha, thank you for Olivia.

I went to Catholic school growing up and that's what my parents are comfortable with. Can the tents be a different shape?

Lawrence is quiet, thinking of the words.

LAWRENCE: They look...Islamic.

MARGO: They're not Muslim tents...Or Islamic (glaring at Lawrence) They're non-denominational tents. (continuing) To finish the ceremony, you two light a Chinese lantern and send it into the sky to symbolize love rising above all...

LAWRENCE: (interrupting) Like real fire?

MARGO: These lanterns have been used in wedding ceremonies for thousands of years. And the Chinese are still here.

CARMEN: One might even say, the Chinese are thriving.

LAWRENCE: (looking at Olivia) I can't offend my parents and then set a forest fire.

Lawrence shakes his head, "No way."

OLIVIA: It's too risky. We just want to get married.

Olivia and Lawrence look at each other, "Forest fire avoided."

OLIVIA: What's the next idea?

CAMILLE: A Buddhist wedding.

LAWRENCE: My parents will flip out if I get married in front of a Buddha.

CAMILLE: There doesn't have to be a giant Buddha.

LAWRENCE: Even a shrine and incense is too much.

Camille accepts defeat, shaking her head, "You're a simple man."

LAWRENCE: Didn't we tell you we wanted a simple church wedding?

Olivia signals Lawrence, "Sensitive zone." He ignores the signal.

LAWRENCE: (freaking out) Were any of you listening? Isn't that what spirituality is about? We just want a simple church wedding.

Samantha, Carmen, Margo, and Camille are quiet.

Olivia keeps signaling Lawrence, ignoring it.

LAWRENCE: (yelling) Is that too hard to plan?

Lawrence is BREATHING heavy, trying to calm down in the awkward silence.

SAMANTHA: (calmly) The last option is the church wedding. And you can have a reception wherever the fuck your family wants.

Samantha glares at him, "Are you happy now?"

SAMANTHA: (even calmer) You simple-minded, male, piece of shit.

Carmen, Margo, and Camille look at Samantha, "Oh no, she's angry."

Olivia is stuck in the middle. She quietly signals Lawrence, reminding him not to enter the "sensitive zone."

EXT. TAI CHI TREE - CONTINUOUS

Samantha, Carmen, Margo, and Camille do tai chi.

They move in sync as the WIND blows.

SAMANTHA: I was so close to using tai chi on him.

Their arms continue circling, slow and graceful.

MARGO: He's an illusion-filled piece of grey dull mass

.

Margo stops doing tai chi as the rest of the group continues.

SAMANTHA: He can fool her, but he's not holding us back.

They stop doing tai chi, looking at Samantha.

SAMANTHA: We're transcending after the wedding.

Carmen takes out her phone, finding the picture

of the remaining cards.

The moon. The universe. The fool.

Samantha, Carmen, Margo, and Camille look at the photo.

They make eye contact, "She's going to learn the hard way."

CARMEN: The cards don't lie.

CAMILLE: Humans do.

SAMANTHA: (smiling) If they want a church wedding, let's give them a church wedding.

EXT. CASTLE CHURCH WITH STEEPLES - MORNING

Samantha, Carmen, Margo, Camille, and Olivia fill the station wagon. Samantha parks in front of the church.

It looks like an abandoned castle.

OLIVIA: I'm sorry he got upset. He means well.

SAMANTHA: We get it. You guys want a simple wedding.

CAMILLE: We got the message.

MARGO: And now we're at our first church.

SAMANTHA: No more emotions. Just solutions.

Margo and Camille look at the church. Unimpressed.

CARMEN: Booo.

Olivia opens the door, getting out of the car.

OLIVIA: Come on, Espiritus.

INT. CASTLE CHURCH WITH STEEPLES - MORNING

High ceilings and rock chiseled pillars surround the pews and altar.

Olivia, Samantha, Carmen, Margo, and Camille's footsteps ECHO through the empty space.

CAMILLE: (calling out) We've come to burn the witch.

MARGO: It feels so...So?

SAMANTHA: Empty.

Los Espiritus look at each other, nodding, "Empty."

Olivia is quiet, sitting in a pew, facing the altar.

OLIVIA: It's too...churchy.

INT. OLIVIA'S KITCHEN - AFTERNOON

Samantha, Margo, Camille, and Carmen design teacher-themed invitations.

They're pocket-sized notebooks with invitations, maps, places to eat, and hotel information.

INT. LIVING ROOM - NIGHT

Samantha, Carmen, Margo, and Camille give the invitations to Olivia and Lawrence.

Lawrence smiles for the first time, flipping through the notebook.

OLIVIA: Thank you, Sammy.

Samantha returns the smile.

LAWRENCE:This is so... (smiling) perfect.

MARGO: We're close.

SAMANTHA: But we still need to find the church.

LAWRENCE: What about the Capitol Hill Church?

CAMILLE: It was too Spanish Inquisition, and not enough Easter.

LAWRENCE: I don't understand.

CARMEN: It needs to be more Easter Bunny and less Zombie Jesus.

Lawrence looks at Olivia, "What do they mean?"

OLIVIA: It's small inside.

Lawrence smiles, agreeing, kissing Olivia's forehead.

EXT. MEGA CHURCH, DAY

Samantha, Margo, Carmen, Camille, and Olivia get out of the station wagon in a mall parking lot.

They look at something. It's hideous.

CARMEN: You can't be serious? I'm saying no right now. It's a Mega Church. They shake their heads, "No way."

OLIVIA: We have to see it. It's the cheapest space.

Olivia walks toward the mega entrance, leaving the group behind.

INT. MEGA CHURCH - DAY

Olivia, Samantha, Carmen, Margo, and Camille walk through a large stadium-styled Church.

OLIVIA: Holy shit.

Big screen TVs hang down from the ceiling.

Olivia, Samantha, Carmen, Margo, and Camille sit down, testing the chairs.

CAMILLE: It's tacky.

SAMANTHA: It's sick.

CARMEN: Gooooo, Jesus!

Carmen stands up, putting her arms over her head, cheering.

OLIVIA: Can you imagine Lawrence and me on the big screen? (announcer voice) Starting for this marriage... OOOOOOOO-lliiivvviaaaaaaaa!!!!

CAMILLE: I want to burn this place down.

Camille takes out a stick of incense, lighting it up. Olivia, Carmen, Samantha, and Margo look at her. Camille waives the incense around, ignoring them. Samantha sees a PASTOR walking around. They disappear from the chairs, fleeing.

OLIVIA: (whispering) What are we doing?

CARMEN: Shhh.

They sneak down a hallway, leading to a door. The Pastor's FOOTSTEPS get louder. Approaching.

The door is locked. Olivia, Samantha, Carmen,

Margo, and Camille search for another exit. They find a hallway.

The Pastor rounds the corner, seeing them.

PASTOR: (calling out) Can I help you ladies? We have mass in an hour.

CAMILLE: He's coming.

Samantha leads them down the hallway.

PASTOR: We have a free meal for seniors after mass.

Carmen stares down the incoming Pastor, standing her ground.

CARMEN: He said the S word.

Samantha grabs Olivia's hand, pulling her away from Carmen.

OLIVIA: (walking down the hallway) Hurry up...

CARMEN: (standing still, doing tai chi) Save yourselves. It's time to practice.

Carmen closes her eyes and takes a deep breath. She sinks into horse stance, arms rising, targeting the Pastor.

The Pastor arrives, catching his breath in front of her.

PASTOR: You're fast seniors.

Carmen's eyes flare as she SMACKS the Pastor with a BACK HAND, transforming to an OPEN PALM FACE strike.

His face crumples in fear.

PASTOR: What're you doing?

Carmen quickly steps on his foot, EXPLODING with a two handed push.

The Pastor FLIES through the air, parallel to the ground.

PASTOR: I'm a m-a-n of g-o-d.

The Pastor SLAMS to the ground, stunned.

Carmen gets in his face.

CARMEN: You can lie to your flock of sheep, but you can't lie to the universe.

Carmen walks away, leaving the Pastor in her wake.

EXT. MEGA CHURCH, PARKING LOT - DAY

Olivia, Margo, Camille, and Samantha are in the car. Waiting.

Olivia shifts around, nervous.

OLIVIA: What was that all about? Tai chi's not supposed to be violent. Carmen is banned from visiting churches with us.

SAMANTHA: I hope she didn't.

MARGO: You know she did.

Carmen exits the mega entrance. She's walking at top speed.

CAMILLE: That's her favorite thing to do.

OLIVIA: Assault people?

MARGO:Terrorize Christians. It's one of her last issues and then she'll be able to transcend.

CAMILLE: There she is.

Samantha drives the station wagon, slowly coasting toward Carmen.

Police SIRENS approach.

SAMANTHA: You didn't...

Carmen jumps into the backseat.

CARMEN: (interrupting) The dragons descended from the mountain.

Olivia rolls her eyes, burying her face in her palms as the car pulls away.

INT. OLIVIA'S LIVING ROOM - DAY

The tip of a pen scans down the guest list, stopping at the end.

Olivia and Lawrence smile, "It looks good." He hands the list back to Samantha.

LAWRENCE: Any luck with churches?

Margo, Samantha, Carmen, and Camille look at each other faking a smile.

Olivia is quiet, shaking her head, "Nope."

OLIVIA: Still looking.

EXT. STATION WAGON - DAY

Samantha parks the station wagon on a side street.

Olivia, Carmen, Margo, Camille, and Samantha pile out.

OLIVIA: Let's make it quick. We've got three more churches to look at.

One-by-one, their eyes find the church's humble, non-denominational entrance. A glimmer of hope. Carmen scans the entrance, settling on the stain glass window. The Lady of Guadalupe holding a sacred heart.

SAMANTHA: I feel it.

MARGO: It's warm.

CAMILLE: Inviting.

CARMEN: This might be it, ladies.

OLIVIA: Carmen, you're on probation. Who's your buddy?

Margo and Camille raise their hands.

OLIVIA: Good. Stay by your buddy.

Olivia leads them into the church.

INT. CHURCH - CONTINUOUS

The walls are simple stone masonry, accented with hand-carved wooden beams.

Samantha, Carmen, Margo, and Camille test out the pews.

CAMILLE: This place has spirit.

They smile, making their way through the church, delighted by the simple details.

Shafts of sunlight, lead them through the pews, across the altar, and out to a garden.

OLIVIA: We're moving. Find your buddy.

Camille and Margo look around, finding Carmen.

EXT. HUMBLE CHURCH GARDEN - MORNING

Samantha, Carmen, Margo, Camille, and Olivia explore the beautiful garden.

CARMEN: It's a Zen garden for Catholics.

An EFFEMINATE PRIEST sits in the middle of the garden, praying the rosary.

Olivia and Samantha approach the Effeminate Priest.

SAMANTHA: Father, what kind of church is this?

OLIVIA: It's so warm inside.

The Effeminate Priest smiles, gracefully.

EFFEMINATE PRIEST: And outside.

Margo smiles, hoping he's gay.

EFFEMINATE PRIEST: As Episcopalians, we accept all God's children.

MARGO: What if we're Buddhists planning a... (looking at Olivia) a Catholic wedding? Are you okay with that?

EFFEMINATE PRIEST:All roads lead home. Do you have a minister or monk for the ceremony?

Samantha shakes her head, "No."

OLIVIA: We can't use a monk. We need a special minister.

SAMANTHA: Someone who gets the...

Samantha moves her hand in circles in the air.

SAMANTHA: Fusion of it all.

The Effeminate Priest smiles, as he makes tai chi-esque circles with his hands.

EXT. STATION WAGON, CITY PARK - DAY

The station wagon pulls up to a large open park. A grove of trees leads to a forest.

Samantha, Margo, Carmen, and Camille look at each other, suspicious.

Olivia texts Lawrence, typing, "We booked the church."

SAMANTHA: I don't see a garden.

Samantha, Olivia, Margo, Camille, and Carmen get out of the car.

MARGO: What if he's messing with us?

CARMEN: Everybody back in.

Carmen does a whipping tai chi move with her hands.

OLIVIA: Calm down. Take a deep breath in...and exhale.

Carmen, Margo, and Camille INHALE slowly, EXHALE calmly.

Carmen takes a deep BREATH in. EXHALES slowly.

Olivia, Samantha, Carmen, Margo, and Camille INHALE together, syncing their bodies and minds.

They EXHALE slowly, getting out of the car.

OLIVIA: Find your buddy.

Margo and Camille put their hands on Carmen's shoulders.

They walk to the forested area in the middle of the park.

EXT. FOREST - DAY

Olivia leads Samantha, Carmen, Margo, and Camille on a trail.

OLIVIA: He's stubborn, but he's loyal. And we're good at dealing with each other. It's practical and convenient.

CARMEN: What about the sex?

Olivia is quiet, searching for the words.

OLIVIA: I'm the sexual one. I think he doesn't need sex

sometimes. Usually I trick him, when he's turned on by research.

CAMILLE: All men need sex. It's like male kryptonite.

The trail leads to an opening. Through the opening, a silhouette moves gracefully.

Samantha, Carmen, Margo, and Camille look at each other.

CARMEN: Part the horse's wild mane.

Olivia looks at the silhouette, "What the—?"

Carmen slowly moves her hands in circles. One hand finishes above the waist, the other hand below.

Carmen peaks through the bushes.

CARMEN: Golden rooster stands on one leg.

Olivia, Samantha, Margo, and Camille peak through the bushes.

MARGO: (whispering) White crane spreads its wings.

They smile at a bearded man with grey hair and young eyes, FATHER ERNESTO, 75, doing tai chi.

SAMANTHA: His Yang style is exquisite.

Father Ernesto turns, seeing five heads sticking out of the bushes.

FATHER ERNESTO: Hello sisters. I knew I felt something beautiful approaching.

Margo, Samantha, Camille, and Carmen melt.

Olivia waves, "Hello," as they come out of the bushes.

OLIVIA: We came to see if...

FATHER ERNESTO: You need a "special" father.

CARMEN: He's psychic.

Father Ernesto holds up his cell phone.

FATHER ERNESTO: I got a text with the wedding date. (Smiling) I'm available.

Samantha and Olivia smile, perfect.

EXT. STATION WAGON - AFTERNOON

Olivia sits shotgun, texting Lawrence. Samantha drives.

The text reads, "We found the church and the Father."

OLIVIA: He's magical. And the church is perfect.

SAMANTHA: Our final mission is almost done.

Samantha smiles at Olivia.

SAMANTHA: (leaning in, kissing Olivia's forehead) Good luck, love.

EXT. OLIVIA'S HOUSE - LATE AFTERNOON

Samantha, Margo, Carmen, and Camille are resting on the couch. Tired.

Samantha is restless. She stands up, doing tai chi as she paces.

Carmen watches her pace, lighting a bundle of sage on fire. Smoke fills the air.

Margo notices Samantha's restless tai chi, breaking out the Tarot cards.

CAMILLE: Right here?

MARGO: (shuffling the cards) Damn right.

Margo hands Samantha the deck of cards.

MARGO: Visualize Olivia smiling and happy. No projecting. Just see her.

Samantha shuffles the cards, calming her mind. She INHALES, deep and slow. EXHALING. Ready.

Samantha cuts the deck, selecting a card.

She hesitates, making eye contact with Margo, Camille, and Carmen.

She turns over the card. It's the Death/Rebirth card.

A SILENCE grows as Samantha laughs to herself.

SAMANTHA: I guess the universe wants me to transcend.

MARGO: If you go, we all go. That's the deal.

CAMILLE: The wedding might change him.

CARMEN: We're here for the wedding.

SAMANTHA: (looking at Carmen, Margo, and Camille) I'm tired. And I'm old enough to know change is a cheap trick. I want evolution. And right now, the only way to stop this wedding is with my funeral.

MARGO: I'm not lying to Olivia.

SAMANTHA: You don't have to. I need Los Espiritus to be with Olivia when I'm gone. If you're not here, she'll run to Lawrence.

Los Espiritus think about it, absorbing the hard truth.

Carmen starts CRYING, setting off a chain reaction of tears across all their faces.

CARMEN: (through tears) What do we tell her?

Olivia's car PULLS UP, PARKING. She's home.

SAMANTHA: (through tears) The truth. I transcended. And you have to plan my funeral.

A car door OPENS. Olivia SHUFFLES, GRABBING boxes, SHUTTING the car door.

Samantha makes eye contact with Carmen, Camille, and Margo.

SAMANTHA: (through tears) It's the only way it'll work.

The tears transform from sadness to love.

Olivia OPENS the front door, holding a large box.

OLIVIA: Are you ladies ready?

Los Espiritus faces, filled with tears, quickly transition to fake smiles.

MARGO: We're so ready.

Los Espiritus nod, agreeing, wiping the tears away. SNIFFLING.

SAMANTHA: We had a moment.

CAMILLE: And it just kept going.

Samantha, Carmen, Margo, and Camille look at each other, nodding, "Just a long moment."

SAMANTHA: And going.

Olivia holds up the large box.

OLIVIA: I got the dress.

Camille, Margo, Carmen, and Samantha CRY louder.

INT. WALK-IN CLOSET, CONTINUOUS

Elegant lace designs take shape as Olivia puts on the dress.

INT. *OLIVIA'S BEDROOM - CONTINUOUS*

Samantha, Carmen, Margo, and Camille wait outside the closet door.

CARMEN: (whispering) Are you sure?

Samantha nods, "Yes."

SAMANTHA: (whispering) We're doing it tonight.

The closet door slowly opens. Olivia steps out, wearing the dress.

She's elegant. A rare treat.

Carmen, Camille, Margo, and Samantha swell with joy, tearing up.

SAMANTHA: You're beautiful.

Samantha and Olivia hug as Carmen, Margo, and Camille give them a group hug.

INT. OLIVIA'S HOUSE - NIGHT

The house is dark.

INT. OLIVIA'S BEDROOM - CONTINUOUS

Olivia spoons Lawrence as they sleep.

INT. HALLWAY - CONTINUOUS

Through darkness, a flashlight beam scatters a moving shadow.

It's Samantha, sneaking door to door.

SAMANTHA:(whispering) Ready?

Carmen appears, nodding, "Born ready."

Samantha and Carmen sneak to the next door, CRACKING it open.

SAMANTHA: (whispering) Margo?

Margo appears, nodding, "Here."

Samantha, Carmen, and Margo sneak to the last door.

SAMANTHA: (whispering) It's time.

No response. She opens the door, finding an empty room.

INT. BASEMENT - NIGHT

A match lights a candle. A circle of candles illuminates the Tarot cards.

Camille looks up, blowing out the match as Samantha, Margo, and Carmen CREEP into the basement.

Samantha, Carmen, and Margo smile, noticing Camille sitting by the circle, holding the deck of cards. Ready.

Burning incense fills the basement as Samantha sits in the circle of candlelight.

Camille, Margo, and Carmen sit around the circle, forming the triangle of Los Espiritus.

In sync, they slowly INHALE, filling their lungs, closing their eyes.

LOS ESPIRITUS: (exhaling) Ommanipadmehum... OmmanipadmehummmmOoommaanniiipaaddmmmeeehhhuuuummmmm... OmmmaaaannnniiiiPaaaDmmeeeehhhhummmmOoommaanniiipaaddmmmeeehhhuuuum-mmmmmmmmmmmmmmmmmmmmmmm...

A trance falls over them. Their breathing slows down...Slower...And slower.

Samantha focuses on slowing down her breath. Slower and Slower, invisible to the naked eye.

Carmen, Margo, and Camille continue CHANTING.

Samantha EXHALES, one last time. Her head slowly tilts up, helping her soul leave the body.

Her breath DISAPPEARS as the candles go out... One...By...One.

Darkness.

Camille, Carmen, and Margo are still, silent, absorbing the moment of transcendence.

A breeze BLOWS through the women as a single candle relights, seeming of its own accord.

SAMANTHA'S VOICE: (V.O.) (softly) Let's start the funeral.

Carmen, Margo, and Camille smile at the lone candle in the darkness.

SAMANTHA'S VOICE (V.O.) (softly) Hurry up.

INT. OLIVIA'S KITCHING - MORNING

Morning light streams through the kitchen.

Samantha's body lies on the floor, covered with a sheet.

Carmen burns incense, smudging the body.

Margo and Camille sit at the head and foot of the body.

Meditating.

Olivia walks in the kitchen, oblivious of the meditation in progress.

OLIVIA: (yawning) Good morning.

Olivia makes coffee: getting a filter ready, spooning coffee grounds into the filter, filling the coffee maker with water.

OLIVIA: I'm making extra.

Olivia wipes the sleep from her eyes, noticing the sheet.

OLIVIA: (laughing to herself) Is this a Buddhist ceremony? (walking away) I'll come back when you're done.

Carmen, Camille, and Margo shake their heads, "You can't leave."

Their faces are sad. Empty.

OLIVIA: What's it for?

MARGO: It's part of the funeral ritual.

Olivia's face wakes up, "Funeral?"

OLIVIA: Are you practicing?

Carmen shakes her head, "No."

CARMEN: She's gone, love.

Olivia looks at them, "Gone."

Carmen pulls back the sheet as Olivia sees Samantha's face. Lifeless.

Olivia, crumbling, stares at the body.

OLIVIA: She was supposed to wait.

INT. LIVING ROOM - MOMENTS LATER

Lawrence holds Olivia as she retreats into his chest. Distant.

OLIVIA: It's her fault.

Samantha's body is still under the sheet in the kitchen.

LAWRENCE: It's nobody's fault. Weddings are stressful.

Olivia glares at Lawrence.

OLIVIA: It's her fault. She chose to leave her body. That's what Los Espiritus do. Remember the video. (Looking at Carmen, Margo, and Camille) Why'd you let her go?

LAWRENCE: They didn't let her go. Death happens.

Lawrence puts his hand on Olivia's knee, consoling.

Olivia looks at Lawrence, realizing what she's lost, turning to Los Espiritus.

OLIVIA: Have you talked to her?

Carmen, Margo, and Camille shake their heads, "No."

LAWRENCE: It doesn't work like that, even if they're Buddhists. You can't talk to spirits.

OLIVIA: It does work like that. (glaring) Even if you're not spiritual.

MARGO: What do you think prayers are?

Los Espiritus nod, agreeing.

LAWRENCE: She's dead. It's over.

Camille, Margo, and Carmen shake their heads in sync, "No, it's not."

CAMILLE: Technically, you're never gone. (Turning to Olivia) She made it out of her body.

Lawrence looks at the body.

CARMEN: Now, we have to get her to the other side.

MARGO: Through the wheel of karma and past the wheel of reincarnation.

LAWRENCE: The wheels can wait until after the wedding. I'll call the funeral home to pick up the body.

He picks up his phone, searching for a funeral home.

Carmen takes the phone out of his hand, "No way."

MARGO: Samantha isn't going anywhere.

LAWRENCE: Samantha is dead. It's just a body.

CAMILLE: According to Buddhist law, it has to stay still.

LAWRENCE: What about the smell? We live here.

OLIVIA: I can live with it.

LAWRENCE: I can't.

CARMEN: The soul lingers outside the body for three days.

LAWRENCE: And the smell?

CARMEN: (ignoring him) And then the soul burns its karma and continues through the wheel of reincarnation.

LAWRENCE: (glaring at Carmen, Margo, and Camille) Three days? Three days of rotting corpse. (turning to Olivia) I'll move it myself.

Lawrence goes into the kitchen, deciding which part to move first, "Head or feet?"

LAWRENCE: I'm not doing it, Olivia.

Lawrence tries to pick the body up by its shoulder. He can't get a good grip. He drops it.

OLIVIA: Stop.

LAWRENCE: You stop.

Lawrence tries again, lifting up the legs, looking at Olivia.

LAWRENCE: Are you going to help me?

Olivia shakes her head, "No."

Lawrence HUFFS, slowly dragging the body from the kitchen into the living room.

LAWRENCE: We're not...
(dragging, straining from the weight)
Leaving...the body here.

OLIVIA: Lawrence, calm down. She just died.

Lawrence turns to Olivia.

LAWRENCE: Oh, now she died. (Shaking his head, upset) I got midterms. I'm chairing two thesis projects. And I'm getting married. (Turning to Carmen, Margo, and Camille) And I'm not a Buddhist.

Lawrence continues dragging the body as the sheet comes off.

He tries to turn the body as Samantha's head SMASHES into a wall.

OLIVIA: (yelling) Lawrence, drop Samantha...and get out of my house.

He's exhausted, looking up. He DROPS the legs, "Fine."

LAWRENCE: (breathing heavily) You're all crazy. Call me when the body is gone.

He grabs his coat, puts on his shoes, and STORMS out the front door.

Gone.

INT. LIVING ROOM - DAY

A bone rattle SHAKES, creating sacred space.

A saffron-gold-lined robe covers Samantha's body.

A Buddhist headdress sits on Carmen's head.

Olivia, Margo, and Camille SHAKE bone rattles.

They sit in a circle, losing themselves in the RATTLING.

CARMEN: There will be a 3-day mourning period. Then the body will be cremated.

Olivia's eyes wander, unfocused. Margo notices.

CARMEN: And we'll end with a wake for extended family and friends. Camille will be the MC and lead the choir. Margo and I will coordinate and run support during the event.

Margo touches Olivia's forearm.

MARGO: You okay?

Olivia is silent, shrugging her shoulders, "I don't know."

MARGO: Take a breather, love.

Olivia gets up from the circle, exiting the house.

Carmen, Margo, and Camille are quiet, waiting until Olivia is outside.

MARGO: Between all three of us, we can barely drive.

CARMEN: What about the Catholic chapter?

Margo and Camille look at Carmen, unsure.

MARGO: The Spirits?

CAMILLE: I can use them in the choir.

EXT. FRONT PORCH - SIMULTANEOUS

Olivia watches Carmen, Margo, and Camille talk through a window.

She takes out her deck of Tarot cards, "I've still got a piece of you."

The wind BLOWS strands of hair into her eyes. She pushes them away.

SAMANTHA'S VOICE: (V.O.) Pick a card, love.

Olivia drops the cards, looking for Samantha. She's alone.

The cards are on the floor as the wind BLOWS one card off the porch.

Frantically, she gathers the cards, putting them in the box.

She looks around, searching for the last card.

Her eyes settle on the tai chi tree. The card is at the base of the trunk.

She picks it up, turning it over. It's the Moon.

SAMANTHA'S VOICE: (V.O.) Remember the moon.

She feels Samantha's presence as the wind disappears.

INT. LIVING ROOM - CONTINUOUS

Carmen looks out the window, checking on Olivia.

Margo makes a phone call.

MARGO: (into phone) Hey, Jen. It's Margo.

JEN: (O.S.) (British accent) Hey, love. Congratulations on the wedding.

Margo pauses, thinking of the right words.

MARGO: (into phone) Samantha's gone.

JEN: (O.S.) (British accent) Like on the honeymoon, gone?

MARGO: She transcended and now we're planning the funeral rites.

JEN: (O.S.) What about the wedding?

MARGO: (into phone) We had to postpone it and now...

JEN: (O.S.) (interrupting) I thought you were going to transcend together. It's safer.

MARGO: (into phone) Plans have...evolved. Do you have a large vehicle?

EXT. SPRINTER VAN - AFTERNOON

Jen, early 70's, grey hair, fit with young eyes, rides shotgun in a Sprinter Passenger van. She's British.

ALEX, mid-30's, tan, casually wearing shorts, a t-shirt, and sunglasses drives the van.

He's cute, even with three-day-old facial hair.

ALEX: Why are we picking up a dead body?

JEN: (British accent) When your mom died, I joined this organization of women.

Alex listens.

ALEX: Like a gang?

Jen shakes her head, "No."

JEN: (British Accent) Like a spiritual group.

ALEX: Do you have turf wars? Catholics versus Buddhists.

Alex takes his hands off the steering wheel, making various meditation hand gestures, mocking Jen.

JEN: Fine. I won't tell you why we're picking up a dead body.

The van swerves as Alex grabs the steering wheel.

JEN: Don't mock the universe. It's always watching.

Alex is quiet, guilty. He focuses on driving.

ALEX: Is this legal?

An awkward silence grows.

EXT. OLIVIA'S HOUSE - DAY

Alex and Jen pull up to the house, park the van, and get out.

They walk up to the front door, KNOCKING.

Olivia opens the door, finding Alex.

Alex makes eye contact with Olivia. She's beautiful.

Jen shoves him out of the way.

JEN: (British accent) Stop getting in the way.

Alex stumbles aside as Jen appears.

JEN: Hello, love. I'm sorry to hear about Sam. (Hugging Olivia) We're here to help.

INT. OLIVIA'S LIVING ROOM - CONTINUOUS

Alex and Jen stand over the body, thinking about how to move it.

ALEX: This isn't legal.

Olivia, Carmen, Margo, and Camille stand by watching.

JEN: Alex, keep your mouth shut. You don't understand what's happening here.

ALEX: Religious freedom.

OLIVIA: Exactly. Samantha wanted a Buddhist funeral.

Olivia smiles, "Religious Freedom."

ALEX: So officially, this makes me part of the spiritual gang. Which makes this legal. (looking at the body) Is this my initiation?

Camille, Carmen, and Margo smile, nodding yes. Jen slaps the back of Alex's head.

JEN: Stop it. We're here to help, and you're not a woman.

ALEX: I was a woman in a past life.

CARMEN: That counts.

Alex smiles, "I'm an Espiritu."

EXT. OLIVIA'S DRIVEWAY - CONTINUOUS

Olivia and Alex carry the body to the van, wrapped in the sheet.

Jen, Carmen, Camille, and Margo open the van doors.

The body is heavy. Olivia slips, dropping it.

Alex catches the body with both hands, sweeping Samantha off her feet.

Olivia scrambles, getting up.

ALEX: (straining) She's heavy.

Carmen, Margo, Camille, and Jen grab the legs, taking the extra weight from Alex.

Olivia joins in, holding up her waist.

MARGO: We're close.

Together, they guide the body into the back of the van. Safe.

Alex catches his breath, closing the back doors.

OLIVIA: I'll ride with Samantha.

Carmen, Camille, and Margo nod, "Of course, love."

Olivia and Alex make eye contact as they get into the van, "I'm ready when you are."

Carmen watches Alex and Olivia.

CARMEN: (whispering) Did you see that?

Margo nods, "Yeah."

Margo smiles, making hand gestures to Camille, "Alex likes Olivia."

Camille's eyes get big.

CAMILLE: Why don't you ride with us Jen?

Carmen puts her arm around Jen, escorting her to the station wagon.

CARMEN: We're going to need a choir, a choir of angels.

EXT. SPRINTER VAN - AFTERNOON

Alex watches the station wagon swerve down the highway.

Olivia rides shotgun.

ALEX: Are we sure they can drive?

Olivia is quiet as they watch the station wagon swerve between lanes.

EXT. STATION WAGON - SIMULTANEOUS

Carmen drives as Jen sits shotgun. Camille and Margo sit in the back.

JEN: (British accent) What do you mean you can't drive?

CARMEN: I was nervous. Alex was checking out Olivia.

Olivia takes her hands off the steering wheel.

CARMEN: Love was in the air.

The station wagon swerves.

JEN: Pull over.

Carmen grabs the steering wheel.

CARMEN: Samantha made this look easy.

EXT. SPRINTER VAN - SIMULTANEOUS

Olivia looks out the window, distant.

Alex notices, uncomfortable. He turns on the radio, finding a station.

Olivia turns it off. Silence.

She's lost in the scenery, holding the deck of Tarot cards.

ALEX: You're a believer in... (funny accent) the Tarot.

Olivia's eyes find the cards in her hands.

She makes eye contact with him.

OLIVIA: I miss her.

Alex is quiet.

ALEX: Jen yells at me, but when she's gone I'll be the first to cry.

Olivia is quiet, looking at Alex. She randomly picks a card with no intention.

It's the moon. She smiles.

INT. STATION WAGON - SIMULTANEOUS

MARGO: Turn right. Turn right.

Carmen flips a switch, but it turns on the windshield wipers.

She flips it again. The windshield wipers turn off.

CARMEN: I can't find it.

Jen reaches over, flipping the turning signal.

EXT. SPRINTER VAN - CONTINUOUS

Olivia keeps an eye on the station wagon as it drifts right, finding the exit.

The van follows the station wagon, heading to the mountains.

Olivia's cell phone RINGS. It's Lawrence.

She pauses, pulling it together, answering the phone.

OLIVIA: (into phone) Hey love, how's it going?

INT. LAWRENCE'S OFFICE - CONTINUOUS

Lawrence stands at his desk, packing up a computer bag.

LAWRENCE: (into phone) I'm starting a new book.

OLIVIA (O.S.) At least one of us will be productive.

EXT. SPRINTER VAN - CONTINUOUS

OLIVIA: (into phone) I'm not Buddhist, but by the end of this I might be.

LAWRENCE: (O.S.) I'll be back from DC in 3 or 4 days... (pausing) And I'm...

The van continues toward the mountains.

LAWRENCE: (O.S.) I'....on....a...mi....you.

His VOICE drops out.

OLIVIA: (into phone) You're cutting out. We're in the mountains. I'll call you later.

INT. LAWRENCE'S OFFICE - CONTINOUS

LAWRENCE: (into phone) I can't hear you. Call me when you can.

Lawrence hangs up.

He looks up at Sophia, smiling.

She smiles back, pulling the handle out of her small red suitcase. Ready.

EXT. SPRINTER VAN - CONTINUOUS

Alex focuses on the road, quiet.

ALEX: Maybe it's a good thing you cancelled it?

OLIVIA: We didn't cancel the wedding. We pushed it back.

Olivia looks out the window.

OLIVIA: I'm getting married.

An awkward silence. He looks at her, lost in the scenery.

ALEX: I was engaged.

Olivia makes eye contact with him. Surprised.

ALEX: Twice.

OLIVIA: Twice? Both women?

Olivia laughs to herself.

ALEX: I knew you'd enjoy my pain.

OLIVIA: What happened?

ALEX: Life. At one point we were right for each other. And then... (remembering) we stopped working on ourselves.

Olivia is quiet, listening.

ALEX:I knew we weren't a good match, but I didn't want to see it. (Laughing at himself) I wanted it to work so bad...I tricked myself.

OLIVIA: Twice.

ALEX: What can I say? I'm a hopeless romantic.

OLIVIA: Were they cute?

Alex is quiet, remembering the women.

ALEX:Goddesses. (smiling to himself) Beth wanted to teach high school English and live near her parents. Find a community. Buy a house. Start a family. The lost American dream. And then there was my Peruvian painter...Mabel. She was ethereal. Too ethereal.

OLIVIA: Like spacey?

Alex shakes his head, "No."

ALEX: I left my body one time and went to visit her. I never told anyone because I thought it was my imagination. When I saw her a couple years later she told me about a special windy afternoon.

Alex pauses, smiling at the memory.

ALEX: She was alone painting and some wind blew open the door. She felt a presence and knew it is was me. She spoke to me in English. I missed her so much, I just wanted to watch her paint. Just share space with her.

Alex stares at the horizon, lost in Mabel.

OLIVIA: That's hot.

Alex smiles, agreeing.

ALEX: She was a soul mate from a past life... (remembering) In this life, we couldn't be together to make up for what happened in the past life.

OLIVIA: What happened?

ALEX: (laughing to himself) Our love was forbidden, and one of us had to die because of it.

OLIVIA: You're lying.

Alex shakes his head, "I wish I were."

ALEX: In the past life, Mabel was forced to watch me... being murdered because our love broke the rules.

Olivia is quiet, taking it in.

ALEX: In this life, we got a chance to meet again, remember the past, and then go our separate ways...living.\

Alex is quiet, thinking about Mabel.

Olivia looks at the cards in her hand, thinking.

She slowly takes the cards out of the box, SHUFFLING.

Alex watches, impressed.

The shuffling STOPS. Her hands cut the deck, gracefully.

Olivia closes her eyes, "Is Lawrence the one?"

She picks a card from the deck, leaving it face down.

Olivia takes a long breath, looking at the upside down card.

She flips it over.

The Hanged Man.

EXT. TAXI - CONTINUOUS

Lawrence and Sophia ride in a taxi.

LAWRENCE: I thought about flying, but I like time to research.

Lawrence holds up two tickets.

SOPHIA: Train tickets.

LAWRENCE: It'll be like time traveling, but we have internet.

Sophia smiles.

EXT. DENVER, UNION STATION - DAY

Lawrence and Sophia walk into a classic brick building with a large 1950's neon sign, "Union Station, Denver."

INT. DENVER, UNION STATION - DAY

Lawrence and Sophia sit on a long wooden bench, nestled between marble pillars.

It's romantic.

LAWRENCE: My new book is on the changing American transportation system.

Sophia listens, attracted.

INT. AMTRAK BORDING GATE - DAY

Lawrence and Sophia give the tickets to a GATE AGENT.

LAWRENCE: I want to use the train to show how a transportation system tamed the American economy.

They walk past the gate toward the train.

EXT. TRAIN - DAY

Lawrence and Sophia walk down the platform, finding their train car.

LAWRENCE: The goal is to parallel it with the rise of the internet and the global economy.

They board.

INT. TRAIN - DAY

Lawrence leads the way down a dimly lit hallway.

He looks at his ticket, checking the cabin number, 8A.

He looks at the cabin door. 8A.

Lawrence smiles, looking at Sophia.

LAWRENCE: (opening the door) We have arrived.

INT. BUDDHIST SHRINE - DAY

Samantha's body rests at the foot of a large Buddha.

Carmen, Margo, Camille, Jen, Olivia and Alex sit, watching the body.

CAMILLE: Now her soul can leave the body.

MARGO: Our presence helps the soul come out.

Alex nods his head, "It makes sense."

CARMEN: She's gonna make it.

Olivia smiles.

EXT. SHRINE - AFTERNOON

Olivia walks outside, texting Lawrence, "We made it to the Stupa."

She erases it, typing it out again.

She erases it. Unsure.

Olivia bites her bottom lip, thinking.

She calls Lawrence. It RINGS.

INT. CABIN 8A. - DUSK

The train cabin is spacious with flip down beds, shelves, a window, and padded seats on both sides.

Lawrence sits on a padded seat, looking through an academic journal.

Sophia watches him read from the other padded seat.

His phone RINGS.

He ignores the call, pushing the silence button.

EXT. BUDDHIST SHRINE - AFTERNOON

Olivia holds the phone to her ear.

It continues RINGING, going to voicemail.

OLIVIA: (leaving a voicemail) We made it to the Stupa.
And now the house smells wonderful.
(laughing to herself, pausing)
Call me when you get to DC.

INT. TRAIN - CONTINUOUS

Lawrence and Sophia smile at each other.

An awkward sexual tension grows.

LAWRENCE: I need some water. Do you want anything?
Sophia looks at him, excited.

SOPHIA: Water is perfect.

Sophia looks through her purse, finding her wallet.

LAWRENCE: Don't worry. It's my treat.

Lawrence smiles at her, exiting the cabin.

Alone. Sophia pulls a pocket mirror out of her purse.

She fixes her hair, inspecting her cleavage, not enough.

She unbuttons the top of her shirt, exposing the perfect amount of boob.

INT. TRAIN HALLWAY - CONTINUOUS

Lawrence takes out his phone, distancing himself from the cabin.

He calls Olivia, continuing to walk through the train car.

He searches for a quiet spot, settling on the men's bathroom.

EXT. MOUNTAIN TRAIL - CONTINUOUS

Olivia sits on a wooden bench, taking in the full glory of the shrine.

Flags waive in the wind. It's peaceful. She's alone.

Olivia looks at the mountains, settling on Carmen, Margo, Camille, Jen, and Alex tai chi'ing by the shrine.

Her phone VIBRATES. It's Lawrence.

She hesitates, not wanting to answer it. But she does.

OLIVIA: (into phone) It's beautiful up here.

LAWRENCE: (O.S.) I wish I was there. The train is crowded. I had to call from the bathroom.

Olivia listens.

LAWRENCE: (O.S.) I know if it was just you and I...

Olivia smiles, expecting to hear what she wants.

LAWRENCE: (O.S.): We'd elope, right now. No guests. No ceremony.

Her smile disappears, "I don't want to elope."

LAWRENCE: (O.S.) Hello?...You there?

OLIVIA: (into phone) I need to get through the funeral first.

There's a pause.

OLIVIA: (into phone) I have to get Samantha where she's going and then I need to find me again.

LAWRENCE: (O.S.) What're you talking about? You are you.

OLIVIA: (into phone) I need more time.

INT. TRAIN BATHROOM - CONTINUOUS

Lawrence stands in the bathroom, putting the toilet seat down.

LAWRENCE: (into phone) How much time?

He sits on the lid.

OLIVIA: (O.S.) I don't know. Two weeks. You don't have to come to the wake. Just focus on the writing.

Lawrence is quiet, "I'm losing her."

OLIVIA: I'll call you after the wake.

Lawrence sadly agrees, nodding, "Okay."

INT. TRAIN CAR, ROOM 8A - CONTINUOUS

Lawrence opens the door, finding Sophia laying on her flip out bed. Reading.

She looks up from the book as he enters the room, finding his eyes.

SOPHIA: Are you alright?

Lawrence is quiet, nodding, "Maybe."

LAWRENCE: Do I look alright?

Sophia smiles, horny.

SOPHIA: You look fine. Where's the water?

He forgot it, apologizing with his eyes.

LAWRENCE: I forgot.

Time slows down as their eyes lock, confirming the mutual attraction.

SOPHIA: (standing up) That's fine.

Her fingers run down the side of his face as the sexual tension takes over.

Their lips and bodies consume each other.

Clothes fall to the floor as foreplay bursts into naked bodies.

INT. BUDDHIST PRAYER HALL - AFTERNOON

A bowl of sand, filled with smoking incense, moves around Samantha's body. Head to toe.

An OLD MONK, 70's, holds the bowl of incense, placing it on the shrine.

The monk bows to Olivia, Carmen, Camille, Margo, Jen and Alex.

MONK: Do you have your letters?

They hand four envelopes over to the monk. The monk smiles.

MONK: Your thoughts will help her soul on the journey.

The monk places the letters under the bowl of incense.

Olivia looks at Samantha's body, tearing up, "Good-bye, love."

EXT. BUDDHIST SHRINE, PARKING LOT - LATER

A long flight of stairs descends from the shrine to the parking lot.

Alex and Olivia walk down together as Carmen, Camille, Margo, and Jen walk behind them. Eavesdropping.

CARMEN: (whispering) They're cute.

Jen smiles.

JEN: (whispering) He's single.

Carmen nods at a bench by the trail.

Margo, Camille, Carmen, and Jen sit down on the bench.

A BREEZE blows through the trees.

Carmen closes her eyes, enjoying the BREEZE blowing across her face.

SAMANTHA'S VOICE: (V.O.) (in the breeze) They're cute.
Carmen opens her eyes, smiling at Camille, Margo, and Jen.

CARMEN: All this mourning is making me tired.

Olivia and Alex stop, looking at Carmen.

OLIVIA: All that tai chi is making you tired.

CARMEN: You guys go. Be young.

JEN: We're going to do a group meditation.

Jen smiles at Carmen.

MARGO: We'll meet you for lunch.

Olivia and Alex continue down the stairs, getting in the car.

EXT. SPRINTER VAN - AFTERNOON

Mountain peaks pass in the rearview mirror.

Olivia TUNES the radio, looking for stations. It's mostly country, Christian talk radio, and mainstream pop.

ALEX: Press the CD button.

Olivia presses the CD button as a soulful instrumental FILLS the car.

OLIVIA: Do you live in Boulder?

Alex nods, "Yeah."

ALEX: I studied at Naropa.

OLIVIA: How Boulder of you.

ALEX: Then I dropped out.

OLIVIA: (laughing) How Buddhist of you.

ALEX: And then...When I found myself... (smiling, looking at Olivia) I studied massage therapy. I have a little office and a group of clients I help through life.

OLIVIA: How's the Boulder bubble?

ALEX: So, you're from Colorado.

Olivia is quiet, smiling.

OLIVIA: It's that obvious.

Alex nods, "Oh yeah."

ALEX: According to the radio, it's a pop-country-Christian-talk-radio state. I think Boulder is doing okay with Buddhist Beatnik poets, farmer's markets, a Google outpost, and legal marijuana.

Alex looks at Olivia.

ALEX: And the gluten free, vegan breakfast burritos are divine.

OLIVIA: I'm getting hungry.

ALEX: Oh look, the Boulder exit. (smiling) It's a sign.

The van exits, passing a road sign, "Boulder, CO."

EXT. BRICK-PAVED WALKING MALL - AFTERNOON

Cafes, local stores, restaurants, and ice cream shops line a pedestrian walking mall filled with people.

STREET PERFORMERS juggle as CHILDREN watch. KIDS play on large bronze frog and turtle statues.

A STREET MUSICIAN plays a fiddle.

A hand slowly moves through space, leading to Carmen's calm face.

Margo, Jen, and Camille do tai chi as Carmen leads.

They're tai chi'ing on a patch of grass as PEOPLE pass by.
Olivia and Alex appear in the crowd, watching them do tai chi.

OLIVIA: They're calm.

ALEX: It's a tai chi trick.

Olivia scans the group, looking for anything suspicious.

OLIVIA: I don't see any strings.

ALEX: Look at their breathing.

Olivia focuses on their chests and mouths, INHALING and EXHALING. Slow and even.

OLIVIA: So what?

Alex mimics their breathing technique.

Olivia notices his slow BREATHING. She imitates his slow breath.

She INHALES slowly and then EXHALES slowly.

She can't breathe that slowly, quickly GASPING for air.

Alex continues INHALING slowly. Unphased.

He smiles, "It's a trick."

ALEX: It's all in the breath.

Margo and Jen see Alex and Olivia in the crowd.

MARGO: (whispering) They're here.

JEN: (whispering) Where?

MARGO: 1 o'clock. Sharp.

Jen scans the crowd, finding Alex and Olivia.

CARMEN: Big finish, ladies.

Carmen moves her arms in a circle as the group follows.

Suddenly, they all jump in the air, spinning in a circle, landing gracefully.
Their hands end in a prayer position in front of their chests.

EXT. BRICK-PAVED WALKING MALL - DAY

Alex and Olivia walk through an open-air mall.

Carmen, Margo, Camille, and Jen flank them.

JEN: How's the new office?

MARGO: We heard all about it in the car.

ALEX: (smiling at Carmen and Camille) We're close.

INT. OFFICE DOOR - DAY

Alex turns on lamps around the office, illuminating plants and crystals, lining the walls.

It sets a dark, spiritual mood.

MARGO: It's like a New Age film noir. I love it.

ALEX: (smiling) Wait for it.

Alex flips the last switch as rainbow light fills the shadows, bouncing off even more crystals.

Carmen, Margo, Camille, and Jen are speechless, enjoying the rainbow crystals.

CARMEN: I'm first. Where's the table?

JEN: You can't volunteer Alex for massages.

CARMEN: I'll pay...for me and Olivia.

OLIVIA: It's his day off.

Carmen steps in front of Olivia, blocking her view.

She takes out some cash, making a face at Alex, "massage her first."

CARMEN: (whispering) This is the real initiation.

Alex smiles hearing the word, "initiation."

Carmen slips him the cash.

CARMEN: (looking at Olivia) You go first, love.

Olivia looks at Alex, "Are you sure about this?"

ALEX: Don't worry. I don't do happy endings.

He opens a door, revealing a small room with a massage table in it.

INT. MASSAGE ROOM - MOMENTS LATER

Incense smoke rises.

The massage table RADIATES soothing music.

Olivia's face pokes through a circular pillow.

ALEX: (O.C.) The body stores trauma over your lifetime.

Olivia lays face down on the massage table.

ALEX: The tight spots.

Alex works on her arm and ribs.

His hands search for tight spots in the muscles.

His fingers stop, pressing in and holding a tight spot in her arm.

Olivia makes a face, "There's one."

Alex holds the tight spot, waiting for it to release.

Olivia SUCKS her breath in, HOLDING it from the pain.

ALEX: Breathe. It's important.

Olivia EXHALES as the tightness leaves her face.

ALEX: The tightness is the stuck emotions.

Olivia BREATHES heavy, recovering.

OLIVIA: Is it gone?

His hands find her shoulder blades, massaging.

ALEX: I found more buried treasure.

His hands press deep into her shoulder blades.

OLIVIA: What does the shoulder blade mean?

ALEX: I don't want to tell you. You might think I'm trying to hit on you.

OLIVIA: (face seizing in pain) Oh no. The pain takes... Aaaaahhh.

INT. MASSAGE ROOM - MINUTES LATER

CARMEN: (face seizing in pain) Ahhhhhh...

Carmen is face down on the massage table.

Her body fidgets as Alex massages her feet.

CARMEN: Do you think she's cute?

ALEX: I need you to stay still and relax.

Carmen stops moving as Alex finds a tight spot in her foot.

Carmen INHALES from the pain, holding her breath.

ALEX: Breathe, Carmen. Don't hold it.

Carmen EXHALES, trying to breathe through the pain.

Alex blushes, thinking of the best answer.

ALEX: Who wouldn't?

CARMEN: Her fiancé. Samantha wanted us to find a replacement.

Alex stretches her ankle and calf as she MOANS from the relaxing pain.

INT. MASSAGE OFFICE/FRONT ROOM - CONTINUOUS

Camille, Margo, Jen, and Olivia hear MOANS coming from the room.

They look at each other, feeling Carmen's pain.

MARGO: She's tight.

INT. MASSAGE ROOM - CONTINUOUS

Alex uses a large massaging device, VIBRATING Camille's hip and body.

It looks like a car buffer for humans.

ALEX: (vibrating) I'm not going to force myself on anyone.

Camille's whole body VIBRATES.

CAMILLE: (vibrating) You were in the cards.

Alex turns off the human buffer. They stop vibrating.

ALEX: What cards?

MARGO: We did a card reading to see if...

Alex listens, while beginning to use a different massaging device. It's a large VIBRATING suction cup.

INT. MASSAGE ROOM - CONTINUOUS

CARMEN: (VIBRATING) ...If they were a good match. The universe always knows. And they were a bad match.

Alex attaches an upside down cone onto the massage device.

He turns it on, MASSAGING Carmen's back.

CARMEN: (moaning) Oh my gooooooddddddd.

INT. MASSAGE ROOM - CONTINUOUS

Margo lays face up on the massage table. She stares off into space.

MARGO: (wincing from pain) They are a horrible match. Exact opposites.

INT. MASSAGE ROOM - CONTINUOUS

Camille lies on her back. She VIBRATES. Her mouth tenses from pain.

CAMILLE: (vibrating) It's like ice cream falling in love with the sun.

The VIBRATING stops as her face relaxes. Smiling.

INT. MASSAGE ROOM - CONTINUOUS

Carmen's face pokes through the circular pillow, laying face down.

CARMEN: It'll never work.

INT. MASSAGE ROOM - CONTINUOUS

Camille lies on her back, staring off into space. Fully relaxed.

CAMILLE: ...Slowly melting...

INT. MASSAGE ROOM - CONTINUOUS

Margo lays face down, face poking out of the circular pillow.

MARGO: Trying to hold on. But it's too late.

INT. MASSAGE ROOM - CONTINUOUS

Alex listens.

CARMEN: The ice cream is gone.

INT. MASSAGE ROOM - CONTINUOUS

Camille is quiet. Sad. Her head pokes out of the circular pillow.

INT. MASSAGE ROOM - CONTINUOUS

Margo stares off into space.

INT. MASSAGE ROOM - CONTINUOUS

Carmen smiles. Relaxed.

INT. MASSAGE ROOM - CONTINUOUS

Olivia's face pokes through the circular pillow. Calm.

Alex adjusts the lights in the massage room, making it brighter, as Olivia sits up on the table.

He puts a new sheet on the massage table. Olivia helps.

They meet in the middle of the massage table.

They're close enough to kiss.

OLIVIA: I needed that.

Alex smiles at her as she hugs him.

The hug is deep as Olivia tears up.

Alex feels the tears, hugging her deeper, letting her know she's safe.

Olivia stops the tears, feeling the love.

INT. TRAIN DINING CAR - NIGHT

The dining car is sparely lit. It's almost empty, except for Lawrence and Sophia sitting at a table by a window.

Lawrence sifts through research on his laptop.

LAWRENCE: This database has photos of the sources.

Sophia watches him. Attracted.

LAWRENCE: The colonial marriage records are scans of

the original documents, but the newspaper articles... (looking at Sophia) You can read the original documents... (eyes searching the screen) Up to 1901.

Sophia smiles at Lawrence, flirting.

LAWRENCE: It's exciting. We have some options.

She leans in, kissing him, embracing the moment.

The kiss is deep and long.

Sophia runs her hand down his pants, fondling his crotch.

Lawrence looks at Sophia, "Here?"

She smiles, slipping down his body, disappearing under the table.

Pants UNZIP as a BLOW JOB begins.

Lawrence smiles, enjoying Sophia's youthful determination.

INT. CREMATION OVEN - DAY

Darkness. Gas FLOWS as a row of flames IGNITES Samantha's body.

Samantha holds the letters from Carmen, Margo, Camille, and Olivia. The letters ignite.

INT. LIBRARY - DAY

Lawrence and Sophia find books on shelves.

They make out between books.

EXT. TAI CHI TREE - MORNING

Olivia does tai chi with Carmen, Margo, and Camille.

INT. SAMANTHA'S ROOM - NIGHT

Olivia cleans up Samantha's room, putting her things in boxes.

A Buddha statue. A meditation cushion. An incense burner. A framed photo of Olivia as a child with Samantha.

EXT. THRIFT STORE - DAY

Olivia donates Samantha's bed and furniture to a thrift store.

EXT. OLIVIA'S DRIVEWAY - AFTERNOON

Olivia takes a box of Samantha's stuff out of the car, walking into her house.

INT. OLIVIA'S LIVING ROOM - AFTERNOON

She opens the box, creating a meditation shrine.

Olivia puts the Buddha statue on a small table, adding the incense burner.

She puts the meditation cushion in front of the new altar.

INT. OLIVIA'S LIVING ROOM - MOMENTS LATER

Olivia lights a stick of incense and puts it into a bowl filled with sand.

She sits in front of the shrine, meditating.

The doorbell RINGS. Olivia opens the door to Lawrence.

INT. KITCHEN - DAY

Olivia and Lawrence sit at the table as he fidgets, trying to find the right words.

LAWRENCE: Something happened on the trip.

She listens, unsure of how things can get worse.

LAWRENCE: I met someone.

OLIVIA: (laughing to herself) She was right. (talking to herself) Fucking cards. (making eye contact) Just leave, I don't want to see you anymore.

LAWRENCE: I wanted to tell you in person. I'm not coming back.

Olivia LAUGHS under her breath, taking off the engagement ring.

She looks at it, slowly giving it back, "Samantha was right."

EXT. OLIVIA'S HOUSE - NIGHT

Lawrence walks to his car, packing up a duffle bag and a suitcase.

INT. OLIVIA'S BEDROOM WINDOW - NIGHT

Olivia watches the car disappear.

INT. CREMATION ROOM - MORNING

Samantha's ashes are collected and neatly funneled into an urn with an ohm symbol on it.

INT. BUDDHIST SHRINE - DAY

The urn is carried down a saffron colored hallway.

It's set in front of a 20 ft. Buddha statue.

Olivia, Carmen, Margo, and Camille sit in front of the statue. Quiet.

Olivia takes a deep breath. Exhaling.

OLIVIA: I'm ready.

Carmen, Margo, and Camille smile. Ready.

INT. WAITING AREA, OUTSIDE SHRINE - DAY

Groups of PEOPLE, all ages and races, wait outside. They're dressed in colorful outfits. A joyful rainbow, ready to help Samantha transcend.

Carmen, Margo, and Camille open the doors, greeting friends and family.
Jen and Alex usher people to their seats.

Olivia hands out programs. Greeting people.

Alex watches Olivia. Attracted. Carmen walks up to Alex.

CARMEN: (whispering into his ear) She's single now.

Alex looks at her, unsure.

ALEX: She's mourning. I'm not that guy.

CARMEN: Look at me. Samantha didn't transcend early to have you mess up the plan. The cards said you're that guy.

Carmen smiles.

CARMEN: And the cards never lie.

ALEX: (smiling back) Humans do.

INT. BUDDHIST SHRINE - DAY

Inside the Buddhist hall, the crowd is quiet as Camille stands in front of the urn.

The SPIRITS GOSPEL CHOIR, a la United Colors of Benetton, surrounds the base of the Buddha statue. Jen joins the choir.

Camille bows her head as the lights dim. Darkness.
An organ PLAYS a slow song as the choir rocks back and fourth.

CAMILLE: Welcome to this moment. This is Samantha's moment. She was the leader of our spiritual gang. And we want to say thank you to all the Spirits and Espiritus who came today.

The crowd CHEERS, CLAPPING.

RANDOM WOMAN #1: (shouting out) We're gonna get you there, love!

RANDOM WOMAN #2: (shouting out) Amen!

Camille raises her hands calming the crowd.

CAMILLE: I'm glad you brought the Great Spirit with you. Because we got some singing to do.

The organ continues into the first song.

CAMILLE: The lyrics are in the program. Let's see if we can get our Sammy through Samsara. (smiling) Espiritus...and Spirits.

The urn is illuminated by a shaft of light from the Buddha statue.

THE CHOIR: (singing) Many rivers to cross, but I can't seem to find my way over. Wondering lost as I travel across the white cliffs of this world, over.

The audience sways, SINGING with the choir.

OLIVIA: (singing, eyes closed) Many rivers to cross, but I can't seem to find my way over.

The organ drops into the full version of Jimmy Cliff's "Many Rivers to Cross."

Olivia watches Carmen, Camille, Jen, Margo, and Alex singing with the crowd, smiling, transcending.

EXT. STATION WAGON - NIGHT

Carmen, Camille, and Margo are asleep. The car is quiet.

SAMANTHA'S VOICE: (V.O.) My ashes.

Olivia drives, focusing on the road, as her hands search for the urn.

She can't find it.

OLIVIA: Carmen?

No answer.

OLIVIA: (louder) Carmen?

No answer. Olivia shakes Carmen awake.

CARMEN: (waking up, singing to herself) Many rivers to cross. Truth is my redeemer.

OLIVIA: Where's the urn?

CARMEN: I got many rivers to cross. Love is my foundation.

Carmen pretends to go back to sleep, turning away from Olivia.

CARMEN: I don't know.

Carmen smiles to sleep. The plan is complete.

EXT. HOUSE OF LOS ESPIRITUS - NIGHT

Carmen, Margo, and Camille walk in the house.

MARGO: I think Samantha made it.

CAMILLE: I know she made it.

Carmen smiles as a phone RINGS. Olivia answers her phone.

ALEX: (O.S.) I bet I have what you need in my hand.

Olivia takes a deep breath, relieved.

OLIVIA: (into the phone) Thanks for being there. I mean here.

ALEX: (O.S.) I can drop it off tomorrow, but I need something from you.

Olivia smiles, curious.

OLIVIA: (into phone) I don't know if I'm that kind of girl.

ALEX: (O.S.) (laughing) I just want you to read my cards.

Olivia nods, "I can do that."

EXT. FRONT DOOR/LOS ESPIRITUS' HOUSE - MORNING

Alex holds the urn, returning it to Carmen.

CARMEN: (smiling) Welcome home, Sammy.

She hugs the urn, walking outside, joining Margo and Camille.

CARMEN: (O.S.) Time for tai chi.

INT. OLIVIA'S LIVING ROOM - DAY

Olivia takes the Tarot cards out of the box.

ALEX: I just want to make sure I'm not missing anything. Maybe my soul wants something and I'm ignoring it.

Alex looks at Olivia. "She's beautiful."

Olivia puts her palm over the cards, filling them with intention. She hands the cards to Alex.

She smiles. Ready.

Alex makes eye contact with her. Ready.

OLIVIA: Think about the thing you're missing. When you're ready, shuffle.

Alex shuffles, closing his eyes, asking the cards and his soul.

OLIVIA: When you're done, fan out the cards in a half circle.

Alex fans the cards into a half circle.

OLIVIA: Choose one side as the head. The other end will be the feet.

ALEX: What do the head and feet do?

OLIVIA: (smiling, mischievous) It's a secret.

Alex points to the left side.

ALEX: That's the head.

OLIVIA: When you're ready, pick three cards that are calling to you.

Alex pauses looking at the head and the tail.

ALEX: It's the head and tail of the universe.

Olivia shakes her head, "Nope."

OLIVIA: It's a secret.

ALEX: Why three?

She shakes her head, "Nope."

OLIVIA: Patience as the universe speaks.

Alex pauses, picking his first card from the middle of the fanned out cards.

His hand floats over the cards, picking a second one.

Olivia lines Alex's cards up face-down from right to left. Face down.

Alex picks the third card. Nervous.

All three cards are lined up. Olivia is ready.
She turns over the first card: the Aeon.

OLIVIA: The Aeon reminds us to look at your life's history and forgive yourself. Then you can create new opportunities through family and career.

Alex listens, suspicious, unsure if the Aeon is a positive or negative card.

ALEX: So...that's good, right?

OLIVIA: We'll only know what it means when we... (smiling, flipping over the second card) ...look at all the cards.

Alex and Olivia look at the second card: the Fool.

ALEX: That can't be good.

She laughs at him. Attracted.

OLIVIA: It means your mind is open and ready to create something new in your career and romantic relationships.

Alex smiles, basking in The Fool card.

OLIVIA: And the final piece.

Olivia flips over the last card: Lust.

ALEX: I knew it.

Olivia smiles, laughing at him.

OLIVIA: That's not what it means. To achieve true brilliance you have to let all of your talents shine. Your radiance will do the rest. Follow your intuition.

Olivia finds Alex's eyes. They get closer. Intuition. And closer, until their lips connect, kissing deeply.

Carmen, Margo, and Camille watch through the window, smiling. Carmen kisses the urn of ashes.

CARMEN: (talking to the urn) Ready, love.

Carmen nods at Margo and Camille, "Let's do it."

They quietly open the door.

CARMEN: Samantha is ready to return to nature.

Alex and Olivia are deep in the middle of a kiss.

They jump up, fixing their clothes, pretending nothing happened.

MARGO: Don't hide it.

CAMILLE: You can't hide it.

CARMEN: When it's real, you feel it.

Carmen hugs herself, closing her eyes.

CAMILLE: All over.

Carmen's hands rub her crotch and breasts, turned on.

MARGO: It's like a fire, burning and burning.

CAMILLE: Yearning for fuel.

CARMEN: You feel the chi, right? Just feed the fire.

Carmen opens her eyes, smiling, staring down Alex and Olivia.

Alex and Olivia are quiet, weirded out, but completely unsurprised and and okay with Carmen rubbing her private parts.

They nod, "We feel it."

CARMEN: Good.

Carmen adjusts her clothes, putting herself back together.

CARMEN: It's time to get our Samsara on.

EXT. VALLEY WITH RIVER - AFTERNOON

A river cuts through a mountain valley. Trees watch over the horizon of endless peaks.

Carmen, Margo, Camille, Olivia, and Alex stand by the river.

Carmen, Margo, and Camille are HUMMING and CHANTING as Olivia and Alex step into the stream. It's cold.

CARMEN: Samantha wanted to be part of the water on earth. This is the last step.

Alex and Olivia walk deeper into the stream. The water is up to their waist.

Olivia looks back at Carmen, Margo, and Camille.

MARGO: (shouting) Go into the middle. It's not that deep.

Olivia and Alex pause, looking at each other, scanning the river for the best direction.

CAMILLE: (yelling) Keep going.

Alex and Olivia support each other through the current and slippery rocks.

The water is up to their chest.

CARMEN: Perfect.

CARMEN, CAMILLE, MARGO: (chanting) Naaam Yooo Hooo Reeen Geee Kyyyooo. Naaam Yooo Hooo Reeen Geee Kyyyooo. Naaam Yooo Hooo Reee Geee Kyyyooo.

Olivia and Alex look at Camille, Carmen, and Margo CHANTING.

OLIVIA: There's the sign.

Olivia opens the urn, ready, making eye contact with Alex.

She pours out the ashes, slipping on a rock, letting go of the urn.

Olivia and the urn float away, lost in the current.

Alex jumps in, floating after Olivia.

Carmen, Camille, and Margo witness the whole thing.

CARMEN: She really wanted out.

Alex and Olivia float down the river, arriving at a shallow sandy area.

Olivia helps Alex stand up as they catch their breath.

OLIVIA: Samanthasara achieved.

Alex and Olivia make eye contact, slowly kissing.

Carmen, Camille, and Margo walk down the bank of the river, finding Alex and Olivia kissing. A GUST of wind blows across Carmen, Margo, and Camille's faces.

SAMANTHA'S VOICE: (O.S.) I made it.

Camille, Carmen, and Margo smile, enjoying the moment.

The wind continues across Olivia and Alex's face.

SAMANTHA'S VOICE: (O.S.) You guys are cute.

Alex and Olivia hear Samantha's voice, smiling at each other.

Margo turns around, hiking back to the car.

MARGO: Let's leave the lovers in nature.

Camille follows her, but Carmen keeps watching Olivia and Alex make out.

Margo returns, grabbing Carmen.

MARGO: Come on pervert. The mission is over.

Carmen, Margo, and Camille disappear into the woods.

Alex and Olivia continue making out...In the middle of the river...In the forest...In a serene valley... Surrounded by mountains.

A perfect nature wedding.

THE END

ABOUT THE AUTHOR

Josh Hyde was born to a Filipino immigrant mother and American father. He graduated in film from Southern Illinois University in 2003. Hyde travelled to Peru to make a documentary on Peruvian shamanism, while interning at Kartemquin Films (*Hoop Dreams*, *Stevie*, *Minding the Gap*). He entered the MFA program at Ohio University, working under Croatian director/producer, Rajko Grlic. He returned to Peru to shoot the short film, *Chicle*, which screened at over 50 festivals internationally (Berlinale, Tribeca Film Festival). This short film was expanded into his first feature film, *Postales* (Edinburgh Int'l Film Festival, Shanghai Film Festival).

Hyde helped shoot and edit the feature documentary, *Sweet Micky for President*, released by Showtime in 2016 (Slamdance Jury Prize, Hot Docs, EdgeFest Winner Best Documentary, Los Angeles FF).

In 2017, Hyde wrote and directed his second narrative feature film, *My Friend's Rubber Ducky* (RiverRun, Sun Valley, Midwest Independent). A year later, he started the *American Filmmaker* podcast focusing on the creative journey of filmmakers from the front lines of storytelling.

Hyde's newest film, *American Hemp*, is a feature documentary following the hemp industry in Colorado for one year.

Hyde is the first American writer/director/editor in the world to publish his screenplays before they're produced, starting with *How to Kill a Bad Man* (Bauu Press, 2018).

He enjoys hiking in mountains, a dry cappuccino, good street food, and chen style tai chi.

OTHER VERY FINE TITLES FROM
TRIDENT PRESS

Blood-Soaked Buddha/Hard Earth Pascal
by Noah Cicero

Marking a significant departure from Cicero's fictional and poetic works, *Blood-Soaked Buddha/Hard Earth Pascal* is a lucid philosophical treatise. Rather than entertain dogma, Cicero approaches a discussion of Buddhism from the refreshing perspective of the everyman, providing a profound spiritual analysis as well as a sharp critique of capitalism. There are even some pretty good ghost stories.

it gets cold
by jasper avery

it gets cold demands a body that is both the haunting and the house, a queerness that is both living and dying. What can be gained by inhabiting this liminal space? What can the inhabitation of dying bring to the living? What can be done when it gets cold?

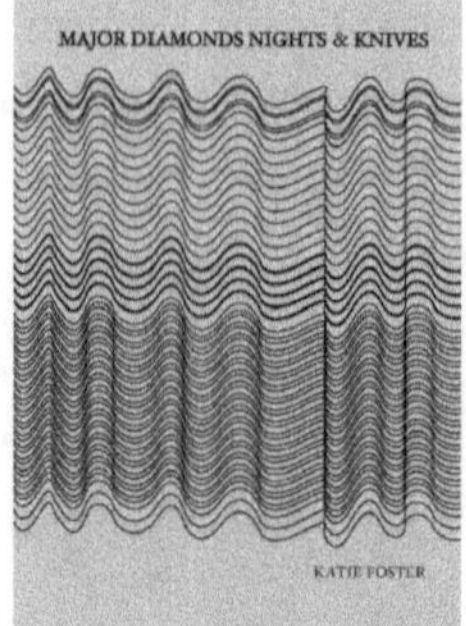

Major Diamonds Nights & Knives
by Katie Foster

Major Diamonds Nights & Knives is a poetry project modeled after a deck of cards. While writing this poem, Katie Foster felt possessed by a spirit who died in childbirth. She tried to tell her story as best she could.

Cactus
by Nathaniel Kennon Perkins

"Shades of Updike's 'A&P' but much less boring." - Bart Schaneman, author of *The Silence is the Noise*

"Perkins does what classic literature does. He invites you to witness an accident, and like the desert, it is beautiful."
- Noah Cicero, author of *Nature Documentary*

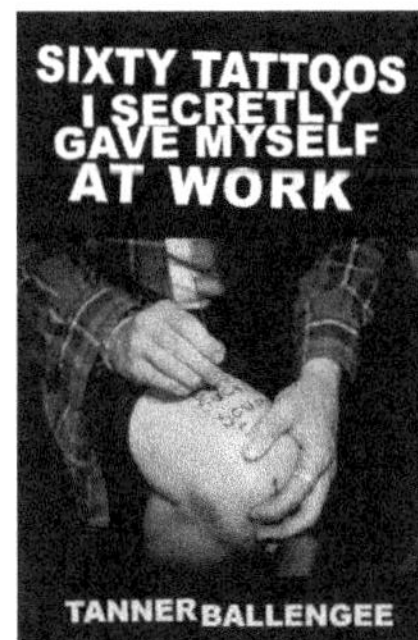

Sixty Tattoos I Secretly Gave Myself at Work
by Tanner Ballengee

Ex-girlfriends. LSD. Motorcycle and canoe trips. *Sienfeld.* Skateboarding. Drunk friends and punk rock and shitty jobs. *Sixty Tattoos I Secretly Gave Myself at Work* is the most beautiful, the most vulnerable of punk and adventure memoirs. Each vignette centers around a hand-poked tattoo that the author gave himself on company time.

The Pocket Peter Kropotkin

Collected in this cute, pocket-sized volume are eight of Kropotkin's essays. The book starts with his indispensable article on anarchism, originally written for the Eleventh Edition of the *Encyclopedia Britannica*, and moves forward to expound on his ideas, which include prison abolition, syndicalism, expropriation, etc.

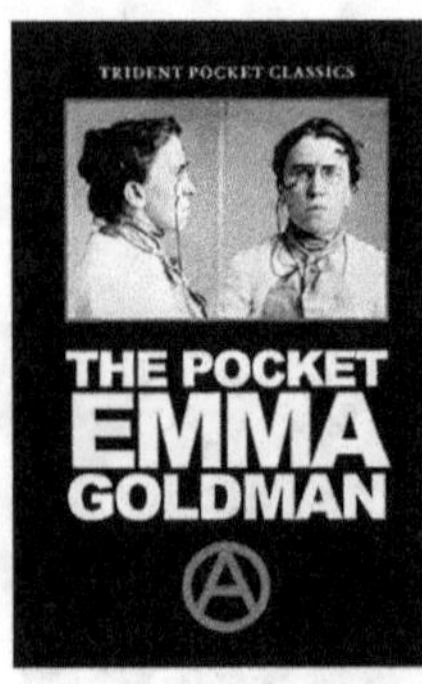

The Pocket Emma Goldman

Some great Goldman essays collected in one place. This book is perfect for carrying in your pocket so you can secretly read anarcha-feminist literature while you're supposed to be working.

The Silence is the Noise
by Bart Schaneman

After a few years living in cities, Ethan Thomas returns to his rural Nebraska hometown and takes a reporting job at the community newspaper. He stumbles upon a big story when an out-of-state oil company pumps enough fracking wastewater into the ground to induce earthquakes. As Ethan learns to write he reconnects with a young woman from his childhood. This is a story about the complicated relationship we have with the places we know best, the pull of the outside world, and finding something to love.

The Pocket Aleister Crowley

Famously called "the most evil man in Britain," Aleister Crowley's impact upon the occult tradition was nothing short of monumental. The selected works contained within this pocket-sized colume offer a way of thinking that is scientific and individualistic, but also deeply mythic and metaphysical, leaving room for both human intelligence and religious inspiration.

Propaganda of the Deed:
The Pocket Alexander Berkman

It was July 23, 1892, and Alexander Berkman was planning to die. He just had some business to attend to first. Dressed in a new suit and a black derby hat, Berkman burst into the Pittsburg office of Henry Clay Frick, the notoriously anti-union manager of the Carnegie Steel Company. From his pocket, Berkman produced a pistol.

This pocket-sized book collects the shorter works of one of the world's most influential anarchists.

The Soul of Man Under Socialism
by Oscar Wilde

"Socialism, Communism, or whatever one chooses to call it, by converting pricate property into public wealth, and substituting co-operation for competition, will restore society to its proper condition of a thoroughly healthy organism, and insure the material well-being of each member of the community."

www.ingramcontent.com/pod-product-compliance
Lightning Source LLC
Chambersburg PA
CBHW070501170726
48291CB00008B/2609

* 9 7 8 1 9 5 1 2 2 6 0 0 8 *